D0546144

**Library and Information Service**

Library materials must be returned on or before the last date stamped or fines will be charged at the current rate. Items can be renewed by telephone, letter or personal call unless required by another borrower. For hours of opening and charges see notices displayed in libraries.

**Lewisham Library**
199/201 Lewisham High Street
Lewisham SE13 6LG
tel. 020 8314 9800
www.lewisham.gov.uk/libraries

3 0 JAN 2013

0 7 MAR 2013          0 8 SEP 2018

2 1 JUN 2015

8/ 9) 2018

9 SEP 2018

Crocus

# Migration Stories

LEWISHAM
LIBRARY SERVICES

CLASS No.

SUPPLIED

INVOICE DATE

**Migration Stories**

First published in 2009 by Crocus
Crocus books are published by Commonword, 6 Mount Street, Manchester
M2 5NS

Copyright © Commonword and the authors 2009

These stories are works of fiction and any resemblance to persons living or
dead or to companies or authorities is purely coincidental.

No part of this publication may be reproduced without written permission
except in the case of brief extracts embodied in critical articles, reviews or
lectures.  For further information contact Commonword.

Tel: 0161 832 3777
admin@cultureword.org.uk
www.cultureword.org.uk

Crocus books are distributed by Turnaround Publisher Services Ltd, Unit 3,
Olympia Trading Estate, Coburg Rd, Wood Green, London N22 6TZ

Cover design by Ian Bobb  ian@axtb.co.uk
Printed by LPPS Limited  www.lppsltd.co.uk

British Library Cataloguing-in-Publication Data: a catalogue record for this
book is available from the British Library.

| LEWISHAM LIBRARY SERVICE | |
| --- | --- |
| CLASS No. | LOCATION |
|  | 15 |
| SUPPLIER | CATEGORY |
| BookScan |  |
| INVOICE DATE | INVOICE No. |
| 28.07.11 | 3953 |

# Acknowledgements

This publication has been supported by the AHRC-funded research project, 'Moving Manchester' (2006–2009), which has explored the ways in which the experience of migration has informed the work of writers in Manchester from 1960 to the present. For further information, and access to the 'Moving Manchester' electronic catalogue, please see www.lancs.ac.uk/fass/projects/movingmanchester.

Thanks to RAPAR for its pathfinding work with refugees.

The Dance, by Muli Amaye, was first published in the magazine *Moving Worlds*, August 2009.

The Container, by Tariq Mehmood, first appeared in edition 32 of *Wasafiri* magazine, Autumn 2000.

# Contents

# Preface

## Before Nations

The story of humankind begins with migration: as a species we fanned out of Africa and settled across the world. Thanks to the advancement of studies in DNA, wherever we are in the world, we can all trace our roots back to those original African migrants.

## Before Border Controls

In the twenty-first century, we exist comfortably with multiple identities. Indeed, if, at the dawn of network theory, we were at only six degrees of separation from one another, that is now becoming five degrees, is becoming four. We are all inextricably linked. How far back need one go along one's family tree to find a branch that is grafted from other shores?

## Before Immigration Acts

Wars, natural disasters, the quest for a life less harsh, provide the impetus for migration. And with these moving people comes a movement of ideas, of ways of seeing, ways of doing. The news that a 16-year-old Iraqi refugee, settled in Sweden, may have found a unique solution to a decades-old mathematical puzzle that has had mathematicians scratching their heads for 300 years is surprising and yet not so. Einstein himself was a refugee. Many of the great poets and artists have produced great art in seeing the commonplace though foreign eyes.

## Before Quotas

The migration stories in this anthology are stories told in the voice of those arriving fresh to UK shores. And yet they are stories as old as the hills, and, if we think hard enough about it, they are the stories of each and every one of us. Sixteen writers from a broad range of backgrounds have told tales as diverse as they are enlightening.

## Before Yarl's Wood

A shipping container is a means of deliverance from poverty and a steel death box. A holiday fling in Iskenderun, Turkey plays out in a café basement in Leeds, Yorkshire. Memories of a South African jazz club still haunt a man 30 years after his arrival in the UK. A Pakistani first-generation immigrant drives his dreams of UK sales success into a wall of failure. A Chinese woman crosses oceans to solve the riddle of a lost love. A Jewish woman from Russia finds revolution in the air during her passage to England.

Those are just some of the stories.

## Before Deportation Orders

I would like to thank the editors, Muli Amaye, Corinne Fowler and Martin De Mello. Their tireless attention to detail helped bring this collection to fruition. And most importantly of course, the authors – without whose generous efforts this anthology would not exist.

Peter Kalu
*Commissioning Editor,*
*Manchester, UK 2009*

# Introduction

## Corinne Fowler

*researcher on Lancaster University's Moving Manchester project*

The comic songs of Victoria Wood evoke some enduring images of Northern England and its industrial past. She sings of 'brass bands ... butties in your hands ... headscarves and mushy peas ... fog, smog, sitting on the bog ... gaslight and games in the street.'[1] Such images make no allusion to migrants. Yet most of the stories in this anthology are about migration to the very places that inspired Wood's songs. It is significant that the stories published in this anthology give prominence to Leeds and Manchester as centres of migration. This is not because the theme of migration has been absent in writing from England's Northern cities. Far from it. It is simply because these cities rarely figure in well-known contemporary English fiction about migration. Despite the proliferation of Northern writing on this theme, especially since the 1980s, such writing has rarely received critical acclaim. Research suggests that this lack of recognition is linked to prevailing popular images of the North.

To portray Northern England as a significant site of migration flies in the face of what James Procter identifies as a national nostalgia for a neighbourly, white working-class North that is 'insulated from' and 'innocent of' the kind of multi-racial society to be found in Birmingham or London.[2] According to this logic, there are no Monica Alis, Zadie Smiths or Meera Syals to be found in the North. But the sixteen  stories in this anthology powerfully contradict the idea that migration has nothing to do with cities such as Leeds and Manchester. For Manchester particularly, migration has been formative of the city and its creative writing. A recent survey by the Moving Manchester

---

[1] David Law first drew attention to Victoria Wood's cultural summary of the North in his PhD. Thesis entitled 'Guddling for Words', 2001.

[2] James Procter, 2006, p.73.

project suggests that the city's literature has been so profoundly influenced by the experience of migration that it would be paradoxical to talk about Manchester's 'migrant writing' as though it could be distinguished from a literary mainstream. Even for those Mancunians who are persistently mis-identified as belonging to a notional 'indigenous white' population, a staggering proportion is descended from Irish, Scottish, Welsh and European migrants. Such claims to indigeneity tend to betray considerable anxieties over the great issues of our time: cultural ownership, belonging and entitlement. The sixteen stories in this collection offer challenging new approaches to such issues.

Fervent, foolhardy, desperate and heroic by turns, the protagonists of these stories journey from cities such as Kingston and St Petersburg, Johannesburg, Tianjin and Lahore. The journeys are frequently unglamorous and often fraught with danger. A notable example can be found in Ovie Jobome's 'The Undertaker', whose protagonist spends a night under 'low wattage bulbs' at a 'Luxury Bus Motor Park' before stepping into a leaky North African boat destined for Europe. Such journeys have been repeated through the ages. Charged with hope, they often end in disappointment. In this anthology, the scenes of arrival tend to be painted in watery browns and slate-greys.

The discoveries that accompany such arrivals pose a number of urgent questions: personal, ethical, political. When the heroine of Valerie Bartley's 'Long Journey to Love' leaves Jamaica to follow a man she barely knows, she has little idea of what Manchester, and marriage, have in store. In Hua Zi's 'Settled for Love', meanwhile, a teacher from Tianjin follows a former lover to Wilmslow where she discovers the true reason why he rejected her. In 'The Rose Seller', a destitute Kurd is forced to sell flowers to Manchester clubbers, while, in 'How I Broke Mama's Commandments' by Sue Stern, a young migrant woman voyages across the Baltic Sea in the company of a Russian revolutionary. The encounter leaves her contemplating the possibility of changing her political orientation, but fate intervenes before she can take a decision.

On top of such trials, many of the protagonists of these stories have to contend with forces that severely curtail their individual freedoms. In 'The Dance', by Muli Amaye, a Nigerian teenager laments the fact that 'as far back as she could remember, official people had decided where she should go, where she should live, which school she should go to.' The unfortunate protagonist of Bashir Ahmed's 'The House Had Many Entrances' struggles to convince the Home Office that his life is in danger if he is forced to return to Afghanistan.

The journeys are not always literal. A fine study of migration's psychological dimension can be found in Martin de Mello's 'When Stories End', which meditates on the memories exported by a song heard by the protagonist thirty years earlier in a South African jazz club. Neither are the journeys always unidirectional. This anthology contains a short story by Qaisra Shahraz, a writer of international renown, whose earlier story 'A Pair of Jeans' was originally published by Commonword before being translated into German and studied by schoolchildren. The characters in her short stories often contemplate the possibility of returning to their homeland yet often discover that the concept of 'home' has a tendency to disintegrate. In this latest story, called 'The Escape', she develops this theme still further. The protagonist, Samir, is as integral to Manchester and Lahore as they are to him. Visiting Lahore as an old man, Samir wonders whether he is visiting his parents' graves for the last time, and he shuttles between the two locations trying to decide where to die. It is often said that the grave is the final resting place. For characters like Samir and Ramesh, the resilient 'English Babu' of Vijay's Medtia's lively story, death is the ultimate act of settlement.

Shahraz's focus on graveyards seems timely at a political juncture when, frequently forgetful of Britain's colonial past, the public gaze is fixed on the nation's forbidden ports of entry. The focus is on the backs of lorries and the undercarriages of the Eurostar. And while the cameras keep rolling over the public spectacle of people without papers, Tariq Mehmood's story reaches into the darkness of a steel shipping container to explore the experience of being trapped inside.

Life does not always end peacefully in these stories. The British Chinese teenager of Rowena Fan's story 'The Son' stands accused of a terrible crime, and violent death is a theme of Matthew Curry's 'The Salesman Saleem'. But, before death, there is survival. In 'Not Wanted', by Maggie Cobbett, Osman follows up a Turkish holiday fling only to end up elbow-deep in greasy pans in a 'squalid Leeds basement'. The story explores the process of adjustment as Osman contemplates the next step. Nor does survival take expected forms, as the young Iranian Farzin discovers in Kathleen McKay's 'Reach'. His redemption from the shock of arrival comes from an unexpected source after a chance meeting with an idealistic dance teacher at the carwash.

# The House Had Many Entrances

## *by Bashir Ahmed*

———

I HAVE COOKED him breakfast and now he is shouting at me. He stands in the doorway shouting. He shouts that he was unable to sleep. His eyes have turned grey like steel balls. He works for ten hours, from eight o'clock in the morning and I scream at night. I have nightmares and I scream in my sleep. He cannot live with my bad dreams. He takes what I have cooked and throws the plate in the bin. He takes his coat from the chair. The pocket is torn.

"You cannot keep waking me up every night, son of a dog. You have no use if you keep waking me up every night."

He puts on his coat and makes his hands into fists. He has large fists. His hair looks untidy. He fingers the torn pocket.

"Wash my socks. When I come back it will be ready and don't forget that."

\* \* \*

This house has two entrances. The house I escaped from had many entrances. The man from the Home Office asked questions like he had something in his mouth, like he was rolling a bullet on his tongue.

"Where did you meet her?" he asked.

I described the house to him in detail. One entrance at the front. A separate entrance for guests. One door at the back leading to the place where they fed the cattle. He was wealthy and he had many good cattle, not lame or diseased. She would feed the cattle so that is where she came out. She fed the cattle on her own. That is how we would meet.

I told him that in our culture when the parents find out that their daughter is having a relationship with a stranger they kill both girl and boy. There is no choice. Even I am alive but she is dead. My family protected me. I have a photograph of her funeral. The women buried her. The women did not want her to die.

I wanted us to be married. I mentioned this to my mother. I told her I wanted to marry the girl and she told me that this could not be arranged. It would be an insult. Her family was a wealthy family and her father was a former commander. We were not suitable. My mother told me this and looked at her hands. They were clean and looked older than she did. We were people who worked on the land. Because of the difference in status my mother refused.

She would feed the cattle. They had one door leading to where they fed the cattle so that is where she came out. Her father when he was a commander killed several members of our Sayed sect. We are all Muslim but we were Sayed sect. We knew the people he killed when he was Mujahidin. We lived all of us in the same village. He had even killed people we knew; we all of us lived in the same village. He had men in attendance who carried guns. Everyone in Afghanistan has a gun. He kept ten or twelve men everywhere that he went who carried guns. She would come out to feed the cattle and that was when we would meet.

The man from the Home Office looked at me and kept rolling the bullet on his tongue.

"When did you meet?" he asked. "When was the first time you met her?"

We met during our relations' wedding. We ourselves were not related. At the wedding people came from the surrounding area. That is the tradition, to celebrate and out of respect. We met at the wedding and from that time I had a friendship with this girl. We met daily sometimes, sometimes every second day. Sometimes for thirty minutes, other times for an hour. She would become nervous and have to leave. She would not look back in case anyone was watching. To her father she was only a woman.

Unless you have lived in Afghanistan you cannot imagine. There is nothing that is the same here. In the village there are farms where there are shelters built for cattle. That is where we would meet. We wanted to talk. We knew of the danger but when you are young you find it difficult to understand what that means. We had not seen anyone killed. The danger was like watching them slaughter a goat. We only talked, we were close to each other, we did not have any sexual contact. Until her brother saw us I myself had not had any problems from her family.

In the past our elders were afraid of her father. He had a lot of weapons. From the time of the Mujahidin he had a lot of weapons. He has fewer weapons now but our elders are still afraid of him. He targeted my tribe. In Afghanistan the tribes fight each other. They live in the same village and they continue to fight. Over a boy and a girl they will fight. Khan Mohammad lost honour. In our culture that is a reason to fight.

Her family attended a wedding. I discovered them on the road. I walked with them part of the way. Her younger brother was with them. I found out they had left her behind. They were kicking up dust on the road and I went to her house in their absence. I remember the dust, watching their progress from the grey dust they kicked. I knew it was safe. Khan Mohammad's men travelled with him. I entered his house and found her on her own. We lay down on a bed to be nearer each other. I remember her face with the sunlight through the shutter. The light looked like a veil. We did not hear her younger brother walk in. We were talking and being near to each other. He yelled and tried to grab a machine gun to kill me. I grabbed hold of the gun and pushed him to one side and escaped. I ran from the house through the village with him chasing after me. He was shouting so that the whole village could hear. The next day Khan Mohammad's men told my father Khan Mohammad had killed her.

All this is the truth but the man from the Home Office had eyes that refused to believe me. They were strange eyes, stiff and empty. His fingers looked soft holding his pen.

"Why did I enter the house and lie down next to her? I knew the danger so why would I do that?"

He did not believe me. I loved her a lot. There is nothing else I can say. I walked six hours to my uncle's house in Surkh Roud. My father came there and told me the girl had been shot. Khan Mohammad: because he is a commander he has a name in Nangahar, so if his daughter or his son does this kind of thing then he has to kill them. He had left a message with my father to bring me to the village. The message was holding a gun. He wanted my father to stand with him and shoot his own son. My father spoke to my uncle and left. Khan Mohammad's men came to my uncle's house and fired a few shots in the air. Khan Mohammad had sent his men to all of my relatives. They warned them not to shelter me. My uncle went out and spoke to them. They said they would come back in the morning.

That night I went to Peshawar. My uncle has a house there. It was half a day's journey in a vehicle to Peshawar. If I had stayed at his house in Afghanistan his life would also have been in danger. Khan Mohammad had been reported to the police. At the district office they detained him not even for one hour. The people who are powerful can do anything. Khan Mohammad is wealthy, he has relatives and friends in the government. I went to Peshawar and stayed four nights before they found me. They paid gangsters to kill me. I returned to Afghanistan.

Every day they came to my father and warned him. They threatened him if he did not tell them my whereabouts. They told my father the Jarga had met and they had made the decision. I stayed in Surkh Roud. My father went to the Jarga and told them that if Khan Mohammad could find me he could punish me. Khan Mohammad said he would cut me to pieces. I stayed three nights in Surkh Roud then left in secret. My father paid an agent to lead me from the country. I left in secret with him on the fourth night.

\* \* \*

I stop remembering. The clothes are in a pile on the floor next to the mattress. If I do not do what I am told they will punish me. It is like I am in jail. The clothes smell of food and of oil and kebabs. The socks have holes in them. I collect them and go into the next room. Bashir has a bed. The other two sleep on mattresses. The clothes in this room are also in piles and smell of sweat. All three of them work hard; they are builders. Their clothes smell of concrete and brick dust. Zabi had left his mobile phone next to his mattress. There is a magazine next to it. I take the clothes down to the kitchen and sort them. I put the dark clothes into the washing machine and leave the light clothes on the floor. My phone rings, Mohammad is calling me to go to their house.

"I must finish washing their clothes."

"You only have to clean, you can finish their clothes this afternoon. Come now, before I must leave.'

I put the washing powder back into the cupboard under the sink and put on my jacket. Why are they treating me like this, I think, as if I am not human?

The clouds are not far from the rooftops. All the time it rains here or the clouds look like they should rain. In my village we could tell how the weather would be from the sky. I cannot tell the weather from the sky here. I cannot tell if the clouds are rain clouds or if it will hail or snow. All the time the clouds are grey like the ash from a cow dung fire, and they are close to the rooftops.

The pigeons look like stones someone is throwing over the houses. Mohammad calls me again and shouts down the phone that I am late. The people on the street are watching me and I feel nervous. Sometimes one of them will follow me so I look over my shoulder. I check no-one is following me or waiting for me behind one of the cars.

The children stop playing football in the street when I pass. They stand and watch me. I wonder why they aren't in school. It still hasn't rained and Mohammad is calling me again.

"I am there now, one minute."

"I have to go now, I'm late. Run and meet me at the door."

I run across the main road and down the side street and arrive at the house. Mohammad is standing in the road looking for me. He raises his hand and calls me a son of a prostitute and then hurries for the bus. I push the door open and walk into the hallway. The house smells of men, of the smell when they don't clean after themselves. I close the door and go into the front room. There are dirty plates on the floor and Coke cans and a plate with cigarettes. Ash from this has been tipped on the carpet. The carpet is old and is stained and it smells. The carpets in all the houses I clean are the same. I collect all the plates and empty cans and take them in the kitchen. I collect the plates from the other rooms. Sometimes there are two or three days of dirty plates. They call me when they have run out of clean plates and I come and clean everything. They have spilt food by the bin. Mohammad phones me again and tells me to cook.

The kitchen is small and the gas cooker is old, very old. In the kitchen they have mouse, because the house is very old and they have mouse and other things, black things. The mouse can eat from the plates. There is chicken in the fridge. Someone has spilt milk and not cleaned it up. All the lino is sticky, you can hear it when you walk. I have tried to clean it many times but the dirt has rubbed into it and it stays dirty yellow.

I cut up the chicken and make chicken biryani When it is cooked and I am ready to leave Habib comes into the house. Habib is a good man but he is quiet and Mohammad treats him badly. He has taken money from him and insulted him for being late to pay his rent. Habib is quiet and can do nothing. Mohammad is a big man, he has status. No-one can fight with him or he will report them to the Home Office.

I ask Habib if he wants food. He was beaten on the stomach before he came to this country and he says that he takes only a little bit of food because of this. He does not want to eat. He looks sick and goes upstairs. I leave to go back to the other house.

Outside I see a police car at the end of the road. They are talking to a Pakistani man with a beard. I tie my shoelace then go the other way. The clouds have fallen apart a bit, there are gaps in them. I walk past the cash and carry. A Pakistani man owns it and all the workers are Afghan. Not the women on the till, they are Pakistani and the man's family. I go in to see if Khalid is there. He is not so I go back to the house.

"You have washed my clothes?"

"Yes."

"What have you cooked?"

"Chana. Chicken curry. We need some more rice."

"You have money for rice."

"No-one has given me money. There is bread."

"You cannot keep waking me up every night. I must be at work early."

"I am sorry."

"No, you must go. You will wake me up tonight. Every night you scream and wake all of us. I don't want you in this house any more."

"But where can I stay? I am not well, I cannot help it if I wake you up. I have too many bad dreams."

He stands in front of me and pushes me to the door. I try to grab hold of the sofa but he pushes me in my face.

"Go now, get out. You can no longer stay in this house. I will not let you stay in this house."

"Please, where can I stay? I am not well."

"I don't care. You are crazy, mental. You are nothing. No-one will help you, no-one will give you work. You are nothing; useless. We work, we have to make money for ourselves. Go then, get out. You will be deported, the British don't want you. Not even your own family. Get out!"

He pushes me in the face again and I try to stop him, I try and block myself from the door but he is difficult to fight. He punches me in the stomach and pushes me out of the door and slams it in my face.

It is dark and the door is shut and I can hear him shouting at the others in the house. I can feel the shadows around me. There is no-one else on the street. I do not know what time it is. Maybe it is twelve o'clock. I cross the main road and walk to one of the other houses and check my phone for the time. It is one o'clock and he had only just come back. I knock on the door of one of the other houses and Ajmal answers. He tells me that he cannot let me in. Firouz has called and told them not to let me in. If they do there will be trouble for them.

Ajmal is a good man but he cannot help me. I try to talk to him but he shuts the door in my face.

I go to the house on the next street. They do not even open the door. They shout through the door at me to go away. I knock louder but they shout at me again and then no-one answers. I keep banging the door until my fist hurts but no-one will open it. I can see the people in the house next door looking out of their window. I feel ashamed and I don't know what to do. I walk to the last house and they tell me to go away. I walk back past the mosque and then walk to the park. It is a cold night but I cannot think of anywhere else to go.

* * *

The park is the one where the pigeons all go. I have seen people feeding them, throwing handfuls of bread. The pigeons smell when there are too many of them. I sit on a bench and look at my phone. It is 1.07.

I feel too cold to stay sitting. I decide to call Jennifer but it is not the right time. The bench feels damp so I get up and walk around the streets. There are one or two cars but no-one is around. I can hear one of the street lights buzzing when I walk again past the mosque. I walk down the road maybe one mile and walk back. All the time I watch out for the police. I am always scared of the police. Everyone is scared of the police. I try to make it look like I am going somewhere in case they drive past. I have only the clothes I am wearing and my phone and nothing else. No-one cares what happens, if I die or if the police take me and send me back to Afghanistan. There is wind blowing sometimes which makes me feel even more cold.

I walk down a side road and then back on the main road and meet a young guy who is drunk. He says to me "Mate, how are you?" and asks me if I have a cigarette. I say no and he staggers away from me. I think he is going to walk out into the road but he comes back from the edge of the pavement. I get back to the park. It is three o'clock and cloudy and starting to get light. I think about calling Jennifer but I sit and watch the sky and feel my emptiness. When I get too cold I walk through the streets again. A cat follows me. I run away from it when it follows me too far. I think it is the same cat that has torn open bin bags that are dumped in the street. They smell of rotten chicken. I shiver and keep checking the time. It is coldest at five o'clock. I cannot stop myself from shivering any more so I phone Jennifer.

"Hello."

"Hi, Jennifer. It's Jawid".

"Oh, Jawid, what's up? What's the matter?"

"I am on the streets. I was pushed out of the house because I wake them up at night."

I tell her my story and tell her I have been on the streets for four hours and I am too cold so please help me. She tells me OK, wait twenty or thirty minutes and she will come. So I wait and she picks me up outside Cheetham Hill Church.

"Jawid, come on, put this on you. Look how cold you are. I'll keep the heating on."

She gives me her jacket to wear and turns the heat in the car towards me. I tell her what happened and I am alone. Then I cry. My father is dead, they have killed him. I don't know what has happened to the rest of my family. Khan Mohammed is a man who has a name and wants to be honoured with blood. I have no-one here in this country, no-one who can care for me. I have heard English people say they feel alone. It is different I think to be alone in your own country. Jennifer listens and I try no longer to cry.

We talk until nine o'clock when the offices open. She phones social services and the Red Cross and Boaz church. Social services say I am lying. She speaks to the manager and he says I am lying, they have seen me before and I was staying with friends. He doesn't believe I was thrown out. Boaz church can put me on their waiting list, but it is a long list. She argues with the Red Cross and keeps phoning back until they say they can help me for one night. She tells her work what has happened but they tell her there is nothing they can do.

"I've been trying to phone Matthew, Jawid, but he's not at work today and his phone is switched off. I don't know if he can do anything but I'll keep trying."

"Okay."

That is all I can think of to say. I have met Matthew I think once. He talked to me in a meeting when everyone else talked to the interpreter. We go to the Red Cross and they give me a hotel room for one night.

# Reach

## by Kathleen McKay

━━━━━

E ARLY IN the morning, there are seagulls even in this most inland
of cities, massing and squabbling so that a person looking out of
a window thinks the whole sky is full of them. Then the sky
lightens, buses start up and early morning workers hunch their way to
work.

*Iran, April 08*

On Monday hospital staff suggested to Farzin's father that he try out
prosthetic feet. He laughed.

'You cannot even get blood for transfusions.'

After the appointment Farzin pushed his father home in the rusty
wheelchair a neighbour had lent them. The wheels squeaked in spite
of oiling.

'Do you want me to take you to the market?'

Farzin's father shrugged his shoulders. They both knew there
would be little there. His father already had the look of a man going on
a journey, the look that his friend Amir's uncle had before the end.

At home Farzin spooned lamb and rice into his father, who
grimaced and pushed away the spoon after a few mouthfuls.

'Enough,' he said. 'Thank you my son, but …'

'You preferred her cooking, I know. Mine is always too sweet.'

*Or not sweet enough* were the unspoken words.

Farzin squeezed his father's shoulder. The older man nodded,
turning his head away, his eyes misting over.

On Tuesday Farzin wrapped his father in a sheet, covering his stumps.
He lay down beside him on the single bed, wanting these last few

hours, and traced the line of his shoulder and arm. His father's body, once so lithe and graceful, shrank and cooled.

Just before dark, Farzin ran to the mosque. Nothing to keep him now.

*Northern England April 08*
In the draughty side room of the dance centre, with empty notice boards showing the evidence of blu-tack and drawing pins, Diane concentrated on the bald head of her department chief. It was still a cold spring. Outside, buds had sprouted and then retreated again as wind and hail started up. 'It'll never work,' he said. 'Why not?' 'Asylum seekers – their lives are too chaotic. Why would they want to dance? They've got other concerns.''So?' 'They won't have the commitment. They won't be able to keep it up.' 'How do you know? We can but try.' 'Let's be honest here. At the end of the day.'This man was such a cliché. You could press a button and set phrases came out of him. 'The bottom line is,' he said. Diane looked at a space between his eyes. 'What's in it for us?''Well, …' and she started on her prepared spiel, tailing off with, 'and we are supposed to be a community college. This is a growth area. It'll enhance the college's reputation.' She could almost see cogs whirring in his brain, and hear cash tills ringing. 'Can you wait outside a minute please while I confer with the other members of the committee? ' One of the other four, a thin, grey-haired woman who had said nothing, looked at her watch. *I need this work,* Diane thought. The cheek of management not putting her up for other teaching positions, saying nobody local would have the necessary experience to teach the advanced classes, that they'd have to look 'further afield'. Who did he think he was, this chief, criticising local dancers as having fat thighs? And him with his fat arse, who'd never been a dancer.

She clasped her hands tight together, like her mother used to do when she was praying.

*Northern England June 08 …*
*Tactile flags*
*Missing cat*

*Leave my fucking car alone, you bastard*
*Try praying*

Farzin lay in bed in Amir's place, thinking over the signs he'd seen in his first few weeks. The first was scrawled in white paint on a paving stone. The second was a photocopied sheet pinned to a telegraph pole, with a weathered picture of a cat.

He'd dutifully written the expressions down, hoping that eventually they would make sense, but the English he'd learnt seemed to bear no relation to how people spoke. All those years of his father trying to drum English into Farzin, teaching him patiently night after night, yet Farzin still couldn't hold a conversation with an actual English person.

'You must go to England,' his father had said. 'London's a good place. If anything happens to me, you go. Promise.'

And before his father, the old-fashioned English their secondary school teacher had taught them. Useless, strange phrases: 'In the first instance'; 'Yours sincerely'; 'Yours faithfully'; 'Your most esteemed servant'; 'Could you possibly?'; 'Would you mind?'; 'No trouble at all'; 'Pleased to meet you.'

That first week he'd spent serving pizza, kebab and chips in the Bigg Market in Newcastle he couldn't understand a word anyone said, but added extra chillies to everything, which seemed to please most. It had put him off pizza for life.

Better here, marginally. At least he was with a friend.

'Come on Farzin, you must get up. I tried everything to get you that job. I, how you say, pulled strings. Don't let me down.'

Amir thrust sweet tea at Farzin.

'What did you do yesterday? You were asleep when I came back from work.'

'I walked into town, to the library.'

'You borrowed something? They have a small Farsi section.'

Amir peered into a mottled mirror, snipping stray hairs on his chin.

'They said I need proof of address. What is?'

'I told you. Remember?'

Farzin shook his head. So many things to remember. He peered through the window. Difficult to tell whether it was day or not. A crow picked at a container perched on an overflowing dustbin. A man with an enormous belly and wobbly thighs walked past.

'And then what else?' Amir began rubbing cream into his thick curly hair.

'I went to the Art Gallery.'

Amir, flossing his teeth now, looked puzzled.

'Yes, it's warm there. I saw, how they call it, "installation"?'

'Installation?'

'Black bags, plastic. A dark room.'

Amir began to laugh.

'Like here.' He glanced at their collection of plastic bags hanging on the bathroom door.

Farzin didn't laugh. Amir had no idea what he was going through. Amir was always so cheerful. Everyone liked him.

'I was thirsty, Amir. I drank water out of the toilets. It's so dry in this city. No fountains.'

'We're not in Iran now,' Amir snapped.

Farzin ignored him.

'No one around except old people and mothers with children. A man began shouting something about the book of Solomon and the book of Jezebel.'

'What did he say?' Amir was smoothing out his trousers, but he was interested, Farzin could tell.

'"Seven years I have been wandering," he said. "Twelve days without sleep." The security guards looked at me as if I had something to do with it.'

Amir jumped up and put on a jacket.

'Sorry. I have to go. Get up. Up, up.'

He pulled the bedclothes off Farzin and dug him in the ribs. Farzin did not move.

'You've had enough time to recover. You are in this country now. You must work.'

'But ... '

'But nothing. You know how to get there?'

Farzin nodded.

Farzin could smell the tobacco on Amir's breath. Amir never used to smoke back in Iran. What would his mother think?

'You can't sit round here for ever. Remember what your father used to say?'

'If you're going to stir shit, be the best shit stirrer you can,' they repeated together.

Farzin's eyes stung.

'Don't cry there, my friend, don't cry.' Amir patted Farzin's shoulders before leaving in a waft of aftershave.

'I will call at the butchers,' he shouted, heading through the door. Amir never bought meat from the market, preferring to walk half a mile to the nearest halal butchers. Not that they had much meat.

Farzin was tempted to put his head under the covers and go back to sleep once Amir had left. Instead, he straightened his bedclothes and fluffed the pillows, trying to focus on the positive. The job sounded better than delivering leaflets, or warehouse work, the only areas open to him without papers. Disappear if anyone in authority came round: get paid half the rate of the English workers, that was the deal in the warehouse. At least at the carwash he'd be outside, with others.

In the bathroom that Amir kept spotless, Farzin shivered under the shower with the trickle of water. He used Amir's aftershave. Amir wouldn't mind, and as soon as Farzin earned money, he'd buy more.

* * *

Diane is in a hurry, so when the young man at the Starwash asks in a bored tone 'Full valet or wash?' she answers without looking up

'Just a wash, please.' But as she sits on the wall away from the spray she notices his dead eyes. Automatically she clocks his movements.

He sponges the car, then hoses it, and finally buffs it energetically. He does a thorough job. He even cleans the wheels. There's something about his manner that alerts her. Potential.

She's been coming here for months. It's a put-together place, with a car drawn on the wall, a list of prices, and a bucket for tips. Nineteen-eighties' rock music blares out, all 'babes' and 'honeys' and 'can't get enough of you', an English the men must learn. A hanging basket with a few straggling geraniums somehow makes the place look even more down at heel. But customers still arrive. The walls, once white, are covered in graffiti, intentional or not, she can't tell. At the side furthest from the road is what looks like a chicken shed, where the men sit when it rains. Behind them traffic roars its way into town.

She watches the man. In spite of heaviness pulling him down (Bereavement? Depression? she wonders), there is grace and economy in his movements. So that when he gravely tells her that her car is ready, as if he is informing her that her dog has been run over, she tips him and hands over a leaflet about the dance class. Up to him. But as she leaves she offers up a wish.

* * *

On Wednesday Amir brings a girl home after work. Farzin can't even look at her. He has no time for all that. Girls love Amir; Farzin had seen the way they stared.

It was obvious Amir wanted privacy, so Farzin put his coat on and went out. As he shut the door he found the leaflet in his pocket, and remembered the small black woman with her Audi. It was cold on the streets, and soon he found himself walking up the hill to the address on the leaflet. The big white cross on the brick building made him hesitate a moment, but the cold wind decided him.

The hall was at the side of the church, or rather former church, because you could see through and there was an empty space at the front, where, he knew, Christians had their altar.

He entered the hall and stood at the back. The teacher let him stay there and join in when he felt able to follow the moves. She ran a fast and furious class. Within ten minutes he was sweating. She told him it was the fourth week, and immediately he felt guilty.

Some of the others looked as if they had been dancing for ever, and carried themselves with grace and pride, moving loosely so that your eyes were drawn to them. Something caught in Farzin's throat.

Near the end of the class Farzin felt the teacher's hand on his neck. She tilted his head up.

'Look forward, not down. Tuck your chin in.'

Farzin lengthened.

'Great work,' she said. 'See you next week.'

As Farzin left, the lights of the city made a circle round the hall, as if crowning it. He smiled, and then realised he had not really smiled since his father's death. He missed him. Curse the day his father made him promise to leave Iran.

'You need to use your English. Make something of yourself,' he'd said. 'See the world. Don't stay here. It's getting worse and worse. Remember Chaucer?' His father was always hopping from one subject to another, and was fond of quoting Chaucer:

'Whan that April with his shoures sote/ the drote of March hath pierced to the rote/ than folk do gan on pilgrimage.' Farzin laughed, thinking of his father's pronunciation. Nobody here spoke like that. Nobody went on pilgrimages.

On the way home he looked ahead, rather than down. He noticed grass, trees and the occasional friendly face.

* * *

Diane despaired the first time she saw the dancers. Floppy arms, hunched postures, gazes directed downwards at the floor, unco-ordinated arms and legs, no sense of timing. But by the evening Farzin turned up, she has knocked them into shape a little. She was determined to make this class a success and show management, especially as the London job had fallen through.

As she leads them through their initial stretches – 'Reach, reach your fingers to the end of the room,' – she recalls her mother's words:

'Girl, you'll have to be better than others. Nothing will be handed to you on a plate.'

Diane stretches along with them, shaking her neck loose, moving her head from side to side. Sometimes she is so tired she never wants to dance again. Or get up in the morning and stretch, and wake up her aching limbs. Or stand in a room and encourage people who'd never danced, using up all her energy. But whenever she feels like that she remembers her parents. She couldn't give up. As long as there was breath in her body she had to keep going and use the talent she was born with.

She starts them on the first foot exercise. *One two three four, rise one two three four, heel one two three four, jump jump jump jump.*

Her parents hardly ever spoke about their early days except on the few occasions they took a drink. Then, under questioning, they would tell her about getting up before dawn every day, both of them working on the buses. At times her mother had to take Diane with her on the 38 bus, if the school was closed at short notice and there was no one to look after her. Diane got a sense of the vastness of the city, mostly full of kind strangers. Even those who weren't too kind, her mother would be charitable about, saying they 'had problems'. The bus had been a temporary home, a place of safety.

She snaps to. How different it was in this small northern city. The people here have no cheekiness, no confidence, they are deferential to authority. That's what she has to teach them: how to stand tall.

Diane takes a deep breath, holds her head high, lengthens and shows them the first sequence.

'Walk, chop, turn, lift,' she says for the fourth week, scanning the class.

'On the four.' The drums start and they begin dancing. She could dance this sequence in her sleep.

Then she breaks the sequence down, and isolates each part. First she concentrates on their posture, then on getting the arms right, then the feet and legs. She makes them walk across the room, and back, prouder this time, eyes lifted.

'Pretend you're the Terminator.' Some look puzzled, so she shows them how, striding across the room as if she owns it, chest out, arms moving in rhythm.

'Others have to move out of your way. Take up space. Act tall even if you're not.' They laugh at her five-foot frame.

Then come basic steps, again and again, with always a bit of play in between to get them to relax, letting them cartwheel across the floor, hop and skip to see who will let themselves go. She slips the learning in and makes them do more than they think they can. The self-conscious ones loosen up and relax, and people encourage each other and clap.

She knows her methods don't suit everyone. She knows that some won't return. But the ones that do will want to be there.

'See you next week,' she'd said. And because Farzin's father had taught him to honour his commitments and not let people down, he goes to the class the week after, and every week after that. It gives him structure, something away from the carwash. During the two hours of the class, he forgets himself. Those evenings he always sleeps well.

\* \* \*

As the weeks pass, Diane gets to know her dancers. There are always quiet ones who might blossom. Farzin is one. He doesn't realise his grace. The first time she adjusts his head and neck to make him stand more upright, he keeps that when he turns up the following week. The first time she stops his arms being floppy, and makes him reach out to his maximum, he keeps that, and more. The spins, the turns, the shunts, the passes, he remembers. And when he does the first back-wards leap and holds a perfect line, looking along his arms without her saying, she beams.

She throws phrases at them: *Peripheral vision. Movement memory.* And they take in the phrases, turn off their minds and learn to trust their body memory. She goes over the moves again and again so that they don't have to think. At times she whispers an instruction in their ear. She never humiliates anyone or makes them feel bad. And gradually they improve, becoming more muscley, more daring, taking up floor space.

Before they break up for Christmas she suggests her idea: a carwash dance. They are enthusiastic and in the New Year start rehearsing. Week by painful week, they improve. She can imagine the final, perfect performance. There's a long way to go, they are amateurs, plodding, with feet on the earth.

'It hurts,' says one, and she wants to tell him about her ballet training: the bloody toes and heels, the pain in her knees and back. Of course it hurts. She carries on pushing them. They get stronger.

\* \* \*

Farzin is at the supermarket he visits once a fortnight to spend his vouchers. It is a Saturday afternoon in early spring. He has bought a large bag of rice and sunflower oil, and is in the frozen fish aisle deciding whether to go for a four-pack or six-pack of white fish when he sees Diane. She's with a younger woman. He is about to say hello when the other woman kisses Diane on the lips. It's not a sisterly kiss, or the type of kiss a mother would give a daughter, but a lover's kiss. The woman puts her arm around Diane and hugs her close. As they reach the till to pay they are still entwined together.

\* \* \*

Winter returns, and, with it, colds and flu. Many of the students are absent. After Farzin hasn't been seen for three weeks, Diane marches up to the carwash to find him. He is sitting inside the chicken shed in the rain, smoking.

'What's this?' He stubs out the cigarette without meeting her eye.

'I didn't know you smoked.'

'I don't. Amir gave me one.'

Amir, a very good looking young man behind Farzin, smiles over.

'I just dropped in. Farzin was a little sad. It's the date of his father's birthday. His father …' Amir lowers his eyes.

Diane puts her hand on Farzin's shoulder.

'I'm sorry,' she says. 'But where have you been?' She knows her manner is brusque, and Farzin looks surprised. Yet she's got no time to waste. The management committee are discussing community projects this week. Her job depends on the funding. She's lied and told the box office she has sold all the tickets she was allocated for the performance.

Farzin throws out his hands.

'A break-in.'

There is broken glass and paper on the floor.

'Looks like you'll have to clean up.'

'Yes.' There is an awkward pause.

'So why haven't you been the class?'

Farzin starts to stammer, and his English gets more fractured.

'Where was I am? What am I to do? I thought I miss much. Not worth come back.'

'And you didn't think to inform me?'

'Sorry. Very sorry.'

'We're working on that new piece, remember. We've only got a few weeks.'

That Wednesday Farzin returns, making sure he arrives early. He is pleased when people greet him. He had thought that seeing Diane would be awkward, but as soon as they start rehearsals he puts everything but dance out of his mind. What he had seen in the supermarket is filed away, to be examined when he can understand it. For now he can't. Diane is his teacher. His father's words are in his ears:

'Our family do not give up. We are not quitters. We keep on trying. Go to England, go. There is nothing for you here. Amir is doing so well in England: follow him, become a success.'

Farzin stretches. Good to dance again. Diane rewards him with a full grin, and makes him work until he sweats.

For the remaining weeks, until the day of the show, she works the whole class hard. When the day itself arrives it is a clear spring evening. No rain. Traffic to town has died down, and the local pub has recently become an Asian supermarket, so there are no longer drunks swaying past the carwash. *Lucky*, thinks Diane.

Passers-by look curiously at the audience assembled on plastic seats and the wall. Some stop to watch. They chatter and laugh before the show, then quieten as the music starts.

When the lights go on, in each corner of the makeshift stage there is a person standing by a car. A woman shuffles on, and creeps from person to person. Everyone but her is wearing a mask. When none of the figures respond, she curls into a ball and weeps.

Then the figures throw off their masks, and leap up and start washing the cars, manipulating hoses with exaggerated movements, pouring water over the cars, polishing and buffing them until they shine. A sun on a stick moves across the sky. A sunflower shoots up. The dancers pat their cars and grin with pride.

Farzin is on stage now for his solo piece. The audience follow him as he jumps and turns and circles, filling the stage, making his body fly. He looks seven feet tall.

In the front row, Diane is fingering the evaluation form management have asked her to give to the dancers. Quietly she lets the pile of forms slide to the floor.

*Do you believe you were*
  a) *Satisfied with the class this year?*
  b) *Very satisfied?*
  c) *Quite satisfied?*
  d) *Not at all satisfied?*
*Do you think you have*
  a) *A good understanding of modern dance?*
  b) *A moderate understanding?*
  c) *No understanding?*

How could you measure and quantify what they'd learnt? Watching Farzin, teacherly pride blooms. She can still see that first dance performance she was taken to, all those years ago in the Hackney Empire, the air full of kids hyper on sugar and excitement. How they moved those dancers. She knew that day what she wanted to be.

Farzin, holding a posture, stretches his arms out above him, and reaches. His fingers point towards the sky. The audience breathe along with him. How far he reaches is the most important thing in the world. They will him on, feeling the tension as he prepares to spring.

'Good extensions,' Diane whispers.

Farzin, his head high, sees patches of blue in the sky. His fingers tingle as he continues to reach.

# The Rose Seller

*by Kim Wiltshire*

FAZIL STARED at the rusted bike frame, then shrugged. 'Can't ride a bike.'

Sam did his double take, the one that never failed to irritate Fazil. 'Everyone can ride a bike. How can you not ride a bike?'

'I'm not everyone.'

'C'mon. It'll be mither without a bike.'

'Why?'

''Cos it'll be proper hard on your shoe leather. Christ! Look, d'you fancy doin' this or not?'

Sam always had these ideas. Sam the scammer. Always full of the next big thing. 'OK, OK,' he sighed. 'Explain it again.'

'Right, what you do is, ride into town, lock it to a lamppost with this proper big chain, 'cos they'll have anything these days. You'll have the roses and the keyrings in here, right, and this card in yer bumbag, right? And a li'l plastic sign, so you don't have to say nothing. And you sell the stuff. Simple.'

Fazil wrinkled his nose. 'Who am I selling to?'

'People in bars. Two fifty for a rose, three for a keyring, a fiver for both. Keyrings light up, see? You get half, I get half. For me capital layouts like.'

Fazil thought about it.

'Don't give me that face,' Sam said.

Fazil looked away and allowed himself a smile. Whatever that 'face' was, it always managed to annoy Sam.

'I mean, your choice, Faz, but right, say you sell twelve roses and three keyrings, then that's, that's…'

'Thirty-seven pounds fifty. If they take the deal.'

'See? That's what, about...?'

'Eighteen pound seventy five each.'

'Oh ... Even so, cash in hand, not bad for one evening's work, eh?'

Sam might call it work, but for Fazil this wasn't proper work. Not man's work. A man should work with some honour, surely? Or for a cause. But Fazil had left all that behind. And now he had to sell stuff on the streets, he'd be some beggar selling stuff no one wanted.

Sam's stupid, encouraging face stuck itself into his. 'I'm trying to help you out here,' Sam said. 'I know you've had a proper hard time of it, least this'll get you back on track mebbe? Eh?'Sam draped his arm around him, encouraging. Fazil had imagined that somehow, once his status had come through, things would get easier, he'd be walking along pavements of gold. But they didn't and he wasn't. No one wanted a Kurd with a Kurdish degree in Kurdish Literature. Surprising, huh?

With a burst of energy, he broke free of Sam's embrace and grabbed the rusting bike. 'Fine, I'll do it! OK? Happy now?''Nice one. You proper won't regret it, I'm tellin' you ...'

Sam's voice faded as Fazil shut the kitchen door on him, 'I'm sure I will, Sam. I've regretted pretty much everything else.'

As he lay on his bed, examining the damp patch that seemed to grow daily, Fazil felt the wash of shame. Why couldn't he ride a bike? He couldn't remember any of his friends ever riding bikes, but he didn't know why. Sam was right, didn't all kids ride bikes? He remembered an old man who rode a bike. Karwan, his father's assistant. Whenever he came wobbling down the concrete road, dust swirling behind him on a hot day, rain turning him the same colour as the concrete on a cold day, Fazil's mother would always say, 'Here comes poor old Karwan!' She would do an impression of him, knees sticking out almost at right angles to his body, one hand on the handlebars, the other holding the hat to his balding pate. 'Poor old Karwan,' Fazil and Kaja would laugh, and laugh and laugh with mother until their bellies hurt. Here was a ridiculous old man coming to do the bidding of an up-and-coming accountant, as his father was considered to be. This old man rode a bike. No one else he could remember rode a bike.But of course he knew things were different then. For a start, his childhood bedroom had been the size of a whole house in England. Nothing like this tiny little 'box room', with its damp patch and nylon carpet with strange orange swirls. The windowsill was only wide enough for the one unframed photo he had of his mother, father and Kaja. When had that been taken? 1992 or 1993? He couldn't remember. By the waterfall near Erbil. He needed to buy a frame for the photo, it was getting damaged from the condensation. He had started collecting books again. So far he had two, both found in a second-hand shop in Eccles. Nothing in Kurdish, but a *Complete Works of Shakespeare* and *Collected Poems* by Wordsworth. They didn't touch the poems of Xanî, but they would do for now. He thought about how little he owned. A few clothes, two pairs of trainers and a mobile phone Sam had found for him, which he rarely used. Who had he to call, except Sam? But at least he had his own room, not like the other boys in the house, a mixture of Polish and Kurdish, but none as educated as him. That's why Sam put him in charge of the house, plus his status. He was legal, and he was Sam's right-hand man.

The clouds breezed past and the rain stopped, started and then stopped again. It was time to go. He checked the key rings were in the front pocket of the rucksack, carefully took the roses out of the bucket of water and put them in the main body of the bag, not doing the top up. He checked that there were several fifty pences in the bumbag. And he read his little plastic card one last time:

> Please I am refugee from Iraq. I am lost all my family and escape torture death. I am Amnesty International support. Please by a rose or keyring. Thank you much for you time.

Sam certainly had scammed this one down to the last detail. Fazil didn't have the heart for it, but he made himself a deal: he'd try it for two nights. If he couldn't take it, he would tell Sam and that would be that. He took the bike through the kitchen and out the front door. He considered trying to ride it, but one violent wobble and he abandoned the idea, instead he began pushing it on the long walk from Weaste to Deansgate.He sensed the night was going to be difficult. He just didn't look foreign enough. On paper he was fine. Kurdish refugee, sorry, educated Kurdish refugee. Yes please! Then when they saw him, he always got the impression they were disappointed. He was fair. Not blond, but crucially, not dark. So he couldn't be wheeled out as part of the equal opportunities policy. Forty-eight job applications and counting told him that. So here he was, trying to earn a few pounds flogging fakery.

Deansgate was buzzing with life, lights and lager when he got there. He locked the bike to a lamppost, and the thought that maybe this wouldn't be so bad crept into this head. People were chatting, drinking, smiling. He crossed the threshold of the first bar. The bouncer looked up and down at him, but didn't stop him. He got out his little plastic card, a lighter and a rose, and chose a target table.The women looked away, the men waved him away. He moved off that table and on to the next but they repelled him too, annoyed at someone interrupting them. And so it went on, some pitying him, some worrying whether he smelt or stole or both. Hands went down to bags, drinks were covered with hands. The next bar was the same, and the one after that, and after that, and after that. He felt beaten now. Panic rose in his chest. He was better than this. His father hadn't sent him to university, hadn't gave him the last of the savings, for this. It was beneath him socially, intellectually, humanly. Men in markets sold, men on streets sold, Karwan's brother sold kitchen goods house to house, or so his father had said. Educated men did not sell. Well, there was his uncle, the farmer, he sold, but then the rest of the family had very little to do with him these days. Fazil walked on, down to Deansgate Locks, and all the way back to where he'd locked his bike up. When he got there, it had gone, just the chain left behind.

It felt as if he'd only just dropped off to sleep when his bedroom door banged open.'Hiya! How'd you get on?'

Sam was in a chirpy mood. Fazil grunted at him and turned over, trying to block him out, but Sam was already going through the rucksack of wilted roses and the bumbag of loose change.'Faz, mate, it looks here like you sold precisely … sod all.''Oh, well done. That is precisely the situation.''How come?''No one wants to buy this rubbish.''But there's no one else in that bit of town. How can you not sell a single bloody thing?' He shrugged. He was tired and wanted desperately to not have a row.'Get these bloody roses in water. They look proper dead.''Later.''This isn't on, Faz.'

Shame crept past Fazil, briefly brushing by. He had to tell him. 'Also, the bike got nicked.'

'Right.' Sam had the wilted roses in his lap and played with a handful of fifty-pence pieces. Fazil couldn't decide if he looked sad, dangerous or both.'I'm sorry. They cut the lock.'Sam shifted, his voice disheartened. 'S'not a mither. I can get another. It just seems like a proper good … you know. We could make a few bob, you know? Anyway, I'm losing money while you're not making any, remember that.''You're joking me?''This room for starters. I could get four hundred a month for this, if you didn't have it.''You could get twenty-five a week, so don't try that, I know more about your finances than you do, don't forget.''Still, I'm just saying, s'all.' Sam sat for a moment, then suddenly jumped up, 'I know, get yer coat. We'll go have a fry-up at Maggie's.'

Fried egg fat dripped into his mug of coffee, but Sam seemed not to notice. His optimism was renewed and he'd hardly drawn breath since they'd come in.'You gotta be a bit more … I'm not saying be proper fake, but you know, act it up a bit.''This was supposed to be easy money?''You've got proper arsey, you have. I think I preferred how you was before.''Before what?''When I first found you. You were on your arse, and you know it.'

Fazil did know it. He wasn't much better off now; even with JSA, he didn't have enough to both live on and send to Kaja to save for her fees. British universities were expensive, but he wanted her over here with him.

Maggie loomed with her coffee pot for Sam and the teapot for Fazil.

'Here y'are, loves. Eh, I don't know how you drink it with all that sugar in it.'

Fazil didn't like to tell her that all that sugar was the only thing that made her tea drinkable.

Maggie banged away and into the kitchen.'You know what you are, don't you, Faz?'

'A flower-seller?' he said, resignedly.

'A snob.''Great.''You didn't want help from that refugee centre, or from that …''I came here to get away from all of that.''All of that, Faz, is life.''Thank you, Doctor Freud. Can we sort out this stupid scam?'

Sam sighed, took a sip of the coffee. There was a gleam in his eye, his 'acting class' gleam.'Right, show me what you were doing last night. Like I was a punter. Here, use these.'

Sam gave Fazil a lighter, a straw, a paper napkin from the table, and shooed Fazil away. Fazil walked to the door, turned, came back and put the three items on the table in front of Sam. Sam looked at Fazil. Fazil looked back at Sam. Nothing happened for a few moments.'That it?''What?'

'That the face you pull? That double lemon – I'm too good for you – sort of face? No wonder you're selling sod all.'

'That's the only face I've got.'

'Sit down. Christ. Now then, watch and learn, Fazil my son. Observe the master.'

Sam took the three objects and went to the door. He turned slowly, a sorrowful look reaching out as if from his very soul as he walked, humble and fearful, towards Fazil, before laying down the three items on the table with gentle reverence.

'How does my face make you feel?'

'Like you might keel over and die at any moment.'

Sam's face snapped back to its usual sprightly joviality. 'See? Proper easy, innit? Bit more effort, s'all you need. Imagine yer whole family've been massacred and yer orphaned sister's been raped by Iraqis.'

'You're not funny.'

'What's that acting? That Marlon Brando did?'

'Saying stuff like that, it's not funny, Sam. Method.'

'Do yer method acting and you'll be right.'

Later in the day, Sam arrived with another rusty bike. And a pile of stinky old clothes.

Fazil took the bike off him but that was all.

'Here.' Sam held out the rags.

'No way.'

Sam shoved them into his arms. 'Sympathy vote. It'll proper get them, I'm telling you. Listen, though, I gotta go, right? Anyone asks about me, don't say nothing. Got something to sort, but I'll be back in a couple of days, OK?'

Fazil nodded bleakly.

'Go knock 'em dead, eh?' And Sam was gone.

That night he wheeled the bike down Liverpool Road, and on into town, past the glassy high-rise flats for accommodating professionals, like him, but ones who could get a job. He read the stainless steel plaques on the office blocks. Accountants, lawyers, financial consultants, life coaches. What on earth were life coaches? If there was ever a need for a life coach back in Sulaimaniah, perhaps he could be the first one? Back home things were getting better, he'd read.

Daynight, daynight, daynight, he lost track of the week. He was doing alright, with his tatty clothes, occasionally pedalling but mostly wheeling the rustbucket v2 between Weaste and Deansgate and back again. Every evening he promised himself he'd try to ride it all the way, and every night some pothole changed his mind for him. He still took it along as a prop. People were beginning to recognise him as he wheeled his rustbucket along.

This evening town was quiet. He locked the bike up outside The

Back Room. He knew it mostly welcomed the type of men he had no time for, and who had no time for him. Not that he was a bigot, in this world he had no right to be.

He was surprised to find a group of women jostling about at the front, trying to get in. Two bouncers draped in black raincoats were refusing them entry, but nodded a hello to him. Yes, he was getting known. It was some type of pre-wedding party, by the looks of them. They were dressed as slightly bedraggled brides. Women seemed to be responding better to him than men, he'd noticed, so he breathed in deeply, grasped his card and flowers, and approached them. The leader of the pack, a tall girl with a plastic tiara that had a bit of net tagged onto it, turned and bumped straight into him.

'Fuckin' hell, what we got here, girls?' The women all turned and stared at him.

'Eh, not bad, not bad. You the stripper, love?' All the women laughed.

Fazil looked to the bouncer.

'Alright ladies, come along, leave our Fazil alone.'

The tall one snatched the card out of his hands.

'Ah, poor lamb, he's one of them asylum seekers. Bless.'

'Fookin' asylum seekers. This rate there'll be no jobs left.'

Fazil flinched.

'Yeah, right, 'cos your Jimmy was saying just the other day how he'd missed out on a job selling roses on Deansgate.' The tall one was standing up for him. 'You shouldn't believe everything you read in the papers. Anyway, I'm the bride, and I like him.'

'Suit yourself, Trace, I'm just sayin'…'

'Well, you've said. So, Farsil, what you up to tonight, love?'

'Er, nothing much. What might you have in mind?'

When Fazil woke up, Sam was sat on the chair. He pulled himself upright and must have disturbed Tracey, because her head turned, she saw Sam and promptly screamed. She had a point. Sam looked barely alive.'What happened, bro'?' Fazil asked softly, when her scream subsided. Sam was reluctant. 'I didn't know you had company, mate. I'll go make some tea.'

Fazil calmed Tracey down, then followed Sam to the kitchen. For the first time in years he'd got laid. Trust Sam to ruin it. 'Well?''Faz, I've made a proper mess of it. Money and shit. I'm sorry.'

Torn between being a good friend and getting back into bed with Tracey, Fazil hovered by the door. The kettle slowly rattled on the stove.'I've lost everything. This house, that house, the one in Eccles. I've lost the bloody lot.'

Fazil watched as Tracey, dressed in her going-out clothes, minus the tiara, crept down the stairs. She blew a kiss at him and was gone.

Great, thought Fazil, things just went from shit to worse when Sam was involved. Then he noticed. Sam was crying. Sam the scammer, cheery Sam, was sobbing gently into his hands. Fazil didn't know what to do. 'Hey, there,' he patted his shoulder. 'It can't be that bad?'

'It's that bad. Not for you though, you can stay here, the new bloke might change the rent, I dunno, but he knows about you. Anyways, I just came to say goodbye really.' Sam thrust himself up, and stumbled out of the back door.

Fazil turned the stove off. He had no idea who Tracey's husband-to-be was, but he was one lucky man. He fell heavily onto his bed, and started to drift off, a half smile on his face. As he drifted, shame crept in. Slow, so slow, it made its way through his books, gently over his photo, still unframed. It weaved through the bamboo patterns in the wallpaper towards his bed, finally over, under and through the bedspread that pressed across his legs. Fazil turned over, closing his eyes so that he couldn't see it, closing his ears so he couldn't hear it. But it was persistent, and it moved into his dreams, into his sleep. What had happened to Sam? Fazil needed to find out. Sam was his friend and needed help. Dammit! Fazil threw the bedclothes back. He chucked his two books, his three trousers, two shirts and his photo into the rucksack and jumped down the stairs. He looked at the rustbucket, but decided against it. This was no time to practise riding a bike.

As he ran outside, he looked up the road. There was no sign of Sam anywhere. Unsure now, Fazil sat down on the wall. The world was crazy.'Fancy a fry-up?'

Fazil startled. Then smiled. He turned to the source of the voice. Sam was stepping from out of a doorway. 'Sure, come on. I will buy,' Fazil said.'Great. I've got nowt left anyway. But, I have got a top idea …'

# Not Wanted

*by Maggie Cobbett*

———

OSMAN FACED the big pile of greasy pans and smiled wryly. His life had come full circle from the little hotel back home in Turkey to this squalid Leeds basement. No, not quite full circle. Here he must keep out of sight, even though he was working harder than ever before in his life. Mrs Sengezer had made it painfully clear that the guests must never be made aware of the poorly paid underlings who cleaned their rooms, scrubbed their toilets and prepared their meals. If it had been so in Iskenderun, he would never have met Liz.

His Liz, who had arrived by bus from Adana late one afternoon. Finding no one on the desk, she poked her head round the kitchen door. Osman knew just about enough English to show her to a room overlooking the Mediterranean and he proudly refused the tip she held out. Amused, she twinkled at him and he thought her beautiful.

He hesitated, encouraged by the way in which she was looking him up and down. Previous approaches by foreign tourists had removed any false modesty about his dark good looks, but none of them had caught his eye like Liz. Knowing that he would be crushed if she turned him down, he could not stop himself asking if he could do anything else for her.

"You could tell me where to eat. Not too expensive. Safe." For a lady all on her own? Was that a hint that she might appreciate some company?

"Iskenderun has many fine places. Maybe I can show you? After work?"

She laughed. "All right. Why not? It's a date." A date! Now he knew that his instincts had been correct.

"Now, what should I wear, do you think?" How many times had he heard his mother ask his father that same question?

"Something pretty." Then he added boldly, "For me." Still no rebuff, so he dipped into his meagre savings and took her to a waterfront restaurant. The waiter knew Osman and smiled at the lordly way he asked for a good table. His new lady enjoyed the prawns and shish kebab, but wrinkled her nose at the Kunefe.

"First time I've had Shredded Wheat with cheese and syrup on it."

"Shredded Wheat?"

"Never mind. Wouldn't have a view like this in Leeds."

"Leeds is where you live? Is it a nice place?"

"Yes. I suppose so, if you like big cities. Very busy. Lots of shops. Wine bars. Clubs. Big university."

They drank raki and watched the sun go down, then went to a small, crowded disco and drank more raki. Soon they were entwined on the dance floor and it was obvious where things were heading. Osman's first sexual encounter had been with a German tourist when he was fourteen and he knew how to please. Liz had come on holiday alone to get over a painful break-up. In a place where no one knew her, the boy's eager attentions soothed her ego. While he was working during the day, he often caught sight of Liz sunbathing or reading and could not wait for their time together. Evenings spent in little cafés or just strolling hand in hand down by the Mediterranean suited them both. So did the long nights of love-making in her room, with the windows thrown open to let in the fresh air and the moonlight. It did not bother Osman that Liz, who generally slumbered until noon, never enquired how he was managing on so little sleep. Quite the contrary, in fact. He preened when colleagues praised his stamina and even joked about Liz taking him home in her suitcase. They could not get enough of each other, so surely something must come of it.

The morning Liz left Iskenderun, Osman told her that he loved her and took a little box from his pocket. It contained a silver ring set with turquoise stones and a note saying PLEASE REMEMBER ME. Embarrassed, Liz said that she loved him too and fished in her bag for something to give. He was delighted with the Leeds United key ring.

"You will write? Invite me to England, yes?"

Liz hesitated for a moment and then said brightly, "That would be lovely."

When no letter arrived, Osman convinced himself that she had lost his address and he decided to follow her to England anyway. His boss, Mr Kasapoglu, caught him painstakingly copying her address from the hotel register and pointed out in no uncertain terms that he would stand no chance of getting a visa.

"We're not in the European Union yet, lad. Even if you *could* scrape up the fare, with no sponsor and no proof that you can support yourself, you'd be sent packing. Better forget about it and get back to the kitchen. You're nothing special, you know. I bet that young woman forgot about you the moment she got back to England. If she'd really wanted to get in touch, she could have contacted you here, couldn't she?"

He had underestimated Osman's faith and determination. A down payment to the local fixer and a promise to send the rest in instalments when he was settled soon had him on his way. He had turned down the *economy* option of being dropped off near a Channel port and trying to stow away in the back of a lorry. The much more expensive *deluxe* route guaranteed safe passage as far as London with a heavily bribed driver.

It sounded ideal, but Osman did not discover until it was too late to change his mind that the heavily bribed driver would only pick him up for the final leg of his journey. Nor did he know in advance that, for much of the time, he would be sharing cramped conditions and bad sanitary arrangements with up to a dozen other young and not so young men. On some days they sweltered and removed as many clothes as decently possible. At other times, they put on everything they had and still shivered. The food Osman had brought for the journey was soon gone and he had to rely on scrambling for his share of whatever the current driver chose to throw into the back. Of

Bulgaria, Croatia, Austria, Germany and France, he saw nothing but the lonely roads where he was transferred from one vehicle to another. One or two of the drivers were friendly, but most were rough types who hissed at him in languages he could not understand. At some stops, crouching fearfully behind whatever load was in the trailer, he heard angry voices and dogs barking.

The heavily bribed driver took charge of him just outside Boulogne and dropped him off a few hours later at a safe house in the middle of a dingy London terrace. Sleeping in a bed again, albeit a hard bunk in a room shared with five other recent arrivals, was wonderful. So were the shower, shave and complete change of clothes for the first time in nearly two weeks. The following morning he was handed an envelope containing the English money pre-arranged by the fixer in Iskenderun and shown the way to King's Cross railway station. Osman had never imagined so much traffic and so many people hurrying along together. His heavy suitcase made contact with several shins as he tried to weave his way through them, stammering his apologies.

"Single or return to Leeds, Sir?"

"Single, please."

A few hours later, he was dragging his big suitcase up Liz's path, happily anticipating her surprise and delight when she opened the door. Her horrified expression cut him to the heart.

"Liz, what is wrong? You are not happy to see me?"

"No! Well, yes. Just very surprised. You'd better come inside."

With the door closed against prying eyes, she told him the truth. A holiday fling hundreds of miles away from home was one thing, but having a nineteen-year-old Turkish boyfriend living with her in Leeds was quite out of the question. She was a teacher, for heaven's sake, already applying for deputy headships, and he was only a few months older than some of her pupils.

"But I love you. We can marry. I will be British. Start a business?" he protested.

"No! That's ridiculous. Look, you can stay here tonight and I'll give you a lift to the station on my way to work tomorrow morning. You'll be able to get a flight home from Manchester or maybe …'"

"Not necessary. Thank you. I will go now." Osman's pride would neither allow him to plead nor to stay a moment longer in a house where he was so obviously not wanted. This stony-faced English-woman would never know what he had gone through in order to reach her. Aching with exhaustion and very hungry, he set off down the road without a backward glance.

His dignity intact, but with precious little else to comfort him, Osman wondered what to do next. Even if he could get back to Iskenderun the way he had come, how could he return a failure and endure the humiliation of asking Mr Kasapoglu for his job back? Or dash his family's hopes? His mother did her best with the little they had, but it was up to Osman, the eldest son, to provide for the family. His mother's pride and confidence in him had shone through her tears as they parted and he would not let her down. How could Liz do this to him! All right. She might have been a means to an end, but he would have done his best to make her happy.

Osman walked on and on, following signs for the centre of Leeds, until he found himself in City Square. He sank down gratefully onto a bench near the statue of the Black Prince. The Queen's Hotel was just opposite and next to that the railway station and the taxi rank from which he had set off so confidently only a short time before. Why had he wasted so much of his English money just to arrive at Liz's house in style? Osman kicked out peevishly at the pigeons squabbling over the remains of a cheese sandwich. That earned him a reproachful look from an old man picking up cigarette ends and putting them into the pockets of his ragged overcoat. Osman closed his eyes to the grey sky and longed for the warm sunshine of Iskenderun. A few moments later, a blast of sour breath made him aware that the old man was leaning over him.

"You all right, son?" The bloodshot eyes were not unfriendly, but they narrowed as soon as their owner heard Osman's hesitant English. "You one of them asylum seekers?"

"Sorry?"

"Own country no good?"

Osman bristled. "Turkey is a beautiful country."

"So why are you here? You a student?"

"No."

"Got any money?"

"Not much."

"Friends in Leeds?"

"No."

"Need somewhere to sleep?" Osman nodded. "I'll take you to a place where you can get a free meal and somewhere to put your head down. They'll pray at you, but they don't ask too many questions."

"Pray?"

"You know." The old man put his hands together and gazed upwards. "To Him upstairs. Leave your case at the station, son. You don't want to look as though you've got too much. I'm Jim, by the way."

Osman reluctantly obeyed, but when he saw the sad queue waiting outside the church his back stiffened. This was not why he had come to England.

"No! I want to work. Find a job."

"Good luck to you then." Osman watched his only friend shuffle inside and retraced his steps to City Square. From there, he set off to make enquiries at the back doors of the many restaurants and cafés in the city centre. His confidence ebbing with every flat rejection, he trawled the area until he could carry on no longer and trudged wearily back to the station. The waiting room looked inviting, but a man in uniform was ordering a scruffily dressed couple to leave and Osman hastily turned away.

So it was that he spent his first night in Leeds slumped in a phone box, hugging his knees to try to keep warm. Stiff and haggard, he went back to the station as soon as it was light to make himself presentable before he set off again on his quest for work. In a few places his enquiries were met with sympathy and even a bite to eat or a cup of coffee to see him on his way. In most, he received only a blunt refusal. His second night was spent on the pavement under the Dark Arches, determined to stay awake in case anyone tried to rob him of the little money he had left. There was not much chance of sleep anyway. The rumble of trains overhead and the constant dripping of water saw to that.

In the morning, Osman counted his few remaining coins and decided that he had been going about things the wrong way. Old Jim had thought that he might be a student. There must be some Turks at the university he had passed on his way to Liz's house. They were bound to know someone who would give a fellow countryman a job without fussing about paperwork.

This was the right thing for him to do. Here he was for the time being, spending long hours in Mrs Sengezer's greasy kitchen in return for room, board and enough money to satisfy the fixer in Iskenderun and send a little home. It was a start. He was making contacts and working hard to improve his English. When his debt was paid, Osman would work even harder to create his own bright future.

# The Dance

## by Muli Amaye

ISSY STOOD with her head bowed and waited. She could sense the shift in the audience as the tension stretched cross the seats. There was a rustling at the side of the stage as the last drummer took his place. But she could only think about one thing as she stood in the thick stage air. The answer was no.

As the first beat of the drum vibrated through the floor and up her slim legs to fill her chest, she turned her head to the left and the right and saw the pity in the other dancers' eyes. They were all thinking the same thing. She knew it. She knew that even as they pitied her, they were relieved it wasn't happening to them. They belonged.

Each time she lifted her head she had to close her eyes as the lights glared deep into them. She wasn't standing in a good place. She wondered if this is how the sun would be when she got off the plane. Would she stand there blinded before hands pulled her away and maybe even handcuffed her? Thumping the rhythm on the boards, she circled with the others. Today she was free.

They'd been practicing this dance for nearly a year. An international dance-off that was being done by some uplink thing, Issy couldn't remember the technical stuff. If they won, it would mean that they could turn professional. *She* could turn professional. They wouldn't be able to send her back then. She was dancing in a British dance group, *British*. Issy would have preferred to do street dance, but someone had come up with the idea that the different countries should swap dances with each other. It was dumb. They'd been emailing each other to create a sense of cohesion. Whatever.

As she shimmied around the stage with the others, Issy thought about the story behind their dance. It was to do with poor villagers and gods and no food or something like that. And how they'd sent their virgins out to plead with the gods. Like there'd be many of them hanging around waiting to do a dance. Issy's heart beat faster as she thought about the two solos she had to do. What if she messed up? What if the gods weren't pleased? She had to do it right. They all had to do it right, they had to win. Issy had to win.

Knowing it would come to this hadn't prepared her. It was like it was happening to someone else. She'd only been eight when they brought her to Manchester, travelling with someone who'd called herself aunty but disappeared as soon as they landed. Issy had looked for her, squeezing between the stinking, sweating bodies that blocked her way, dodging the hands that would have slapped her, ignoring the shouts from scary old men. But the crowds thinned out and she still couldn't find aunty. She was on her own and she was scared.

Pushing out her arms, she flexed her body in time to the beat. The heat was rising now and she could feel the sweat trickling between her shoulder blades. Dipping low she snaked her body upwards. It was a policewoman who'd come and taken her to a small grey room. She'd eaten doughnuts while she waited, covered in icing with pink and white flakes. That was the first time she'd ever tasted them. Back to back now, she sidestepped, bumping backsides and shoulder blades before taking one step forward.

Issy had lived here longer than she'd lived in Nigeria. This was her home. She didn't know her parents or her brothers and sisters. Her social worker had told her a few weeks ago that they'd managed to make contact. That she had a large family waiting for her back home. And how exciting was that? It was bullshit and they both knew it. Manchester was Issy's home. This was where she belonged.

Breathing deeply, she waited at the left-hand side of the stage for her first solo. They each took centre stage at different points throughout the dance. Issy was third. She kept her eyes fixed to the boards in front of her. It wasn't supposed to have been like that. Aunty should have passed her over to some guy waiting at the barrier when they came through. But something had gone wrong. The social worker said aunty had probably panicked. Maybe it was her first time, or maybe it had been the plan all along, they'd never know. But the fact was, Issy was abandoned at the airport with no passport. The music altered as the soloist shimmied around the stage. She'd been taken to the emergency unit. Issy could still remember it. The low flat building had reminded her of the chief's house in her village. The thought startled her and she stumbled slightly. She didn't know she'd remembered that. The second soloist took her place and a new rhythm vibrated around the theatre. There were too many corridors and glass doors and the boys had made fun of her. They spoke too fast and she couldn't understand them. Issy had cried for a long time. There was one lady, Jackie, who'd sat with her and held her hand. She was the nicest. And when she'd learnt enough England-English to understand what was going on, Jackie had warned her about the men that hung around outside. Had told her not to go out alone. That was a laugh. She could come all the way from Nigeria on her own but she couldn't go out the door of the place she was living. She'd been there for six months before they found her a family to live with. The tempo increased and Issy lunged across the stage throwing her arms forward and following with her body. Her feet moved in staccato and her hips twirled in a frenzy as she took centre stage.

Her parents had sent her to work for some rich African family. She'd been bought, apparently. They'd received money for their eldest daughter. How could they do that? The lady who came from the refugee place had told her; when she was about due to do her year GCSEs. Her own parents had sold her. Pushing her chest out, Issy thumped out the beat, her breath becoming shallow. She'd tried to make it sound normal, the refugee woman, a thing that happened with poor families in her country, but Issy wouldn't listen. She hated them. They had no right to do that to her. She'd said that her parents wouldn't have known, perhaps they were paying a debt, perhaps they'd been promised a better life for Issy, with regular money being sent home. Perhaps it had been Issy's duty to do this for her family. Like fuck it was. Would she send her own daughter to another country if she needed some dosh? The music froze and Issy held her pose before the drum beat started again, softer this time and she shimmied to the back of the stage while another dancer took her place.

Breathing heavily now, Issy waited for her body to calm down. The sweat was pouring into her eyes. They were stinging. She wiped around her mascara with the tips of her fingers. She could look out from where she was now, in the shadows. The audience was vague shapes rising like a tidal wave. To the left she could see her teacher moving in time to the beat. Two more solos to go.

The foster families were mostly ok. But luckily her first social worker had liked her and had worked really hard to find her somewhere she could stay long term. It had taken five attempts before she'd been put with Molly, who cooked rice and peas and stew beans and mutton and oxtail. She'd stayed there until she was sixteen, had been part of the family. But then she'd had to move on. Those three years she'd spent with Molly and her family had been almost like belonging. But each time the family went on holiday she'd been placed somewhere else because Molly couldn't get her a passport so she could go with them.

Manchester Foyer had been the place to begin her independence. They'd meant it was the place for her to get used to being alone. The beat changed again as the solo dancers changed. It wouldn't be long now until Issy danced the finale. Her final plea to the faceless gods. It had been ok living there. She'd worked her way up to the top floor because she went to college every day, and didn't do drugs. She didn't even drink much. She couldn't if she wanted to take her dancing seriously. Her mate had introduced her to a guy who said he could help. Issy hadn't even known she needed help then. But it worked out she did. That she was being watched by the Home Office or something. She'd laughed when he said that. As if. As if anyone was interested in what she did. But he was serious. Said she was a foreigner. That she'd be sent home when she got to eighteen.

Her body was cooling down now. She stood in the shadows and waited for her final entrance. She'd chosen not to let the man help her.

She didn't trust him. Had heard the stories of girls ending up as prostitutes and shit, and there was no way that was gonna be her life. Her mates had turned against her a bit after that, said she was a snob, that she deserved to be sent back, that she'd change her mind. Issy had trusted her solicitor. She'd trusted the system. And it was like they'd both screwed her. The beat was picking up now, this was the part of the dance where the gods weren't happy and the drums were loud and the lights were flashing. The girls on stage were vibrating with the music, coming together and pushing apart. Issy had so looked forward to this bit. Hers was the main part.

As the music went lower, only for a few bars, Issy could feel the audience preparing to do something. She could feel the shift in their posture as arms were unfolded and hands were freed from pockets ready to applaud. This was the part she liked the best. This was when they were pushed back into their seats as the drumbeat became ferocious. The gods were displeased with the dances that had been offered. Now the group had to re-form, make an offering to appease them. Issy could feel the rhythm pulsing through her body her heart beating longer and harder as the drum became part of her. Stomping in time, the girls came together in the middle of the stage. Pushing against each other they acted out the displeasure of the gods until the music felled them one by one and only Issy was left standing, head bowed, hands held out in supplication. If only, she thought as she raised her head and her arms, if only she could go in front of the judge herself and tell him.

Stepping away from the prostrate girls, Issy moved to the front of the stage. The drums were now a rumble in the background, the lights soft behind her. As the spotlight slowly brightened she began to appease the angry gods, to dance for their lives.

Standing at the front of the stage she felt her foreignness pulling her down, the bureaucracy wrapping itself around her like African cloth. As far back as she could remember, official people had decided where she should go, where she should live, which school she should go to. Issy had had enough. She twirled around the stage alternatively bowing and preening, seducing the gods with a flick of her hips while looking demurely downwards, looking boldly forward, covering her body with her hands. Spreading her arms, she twirled and dipped, pulsing her thin body to the beat of the drums, oblivious to everything except the rhythm running through her.

As the drumming slowed down and she reached centre stage, joining the other girls in a victory pose, Issy thought about her solicitor's last message. *Now we can appeal.*

# The Son

*by Rowena Fan*

---

**Catherine**

'Well Miss Byrne? From the top?'

She tucked a strand of brown hair behind her ear.

'I'm not sure. It was quick. It happened in detention. One of the other boys, Rupert Wu was the person, apparently.'

'Apparently, Miss Byrne?' he stopped, placing his pen down beside his stained coffee mug.

'Catherine. You have to consider the greater good. What works for you, what works for the school, and what works for these boys', he said, furrowing his brow.

'But I think it was an accident. A horrible accident.'

'The police will be coming shortly.'

Outside the school bell rang; a loud shrill tone that shook her chair. She wished she were a pupil too; free to run to the playground.

'Yesterday, I kept two boys, Dillon Jackson and Rupert Wu, for detention. Rupert Wu did not do his science homework I'd set last week. Dillon Jackson had been misbehaving throughout the lesson. He was throwing things at other pupils, so I gave him detention too. They were to sit after class for ten minutes. Six minutes in, they started to fight. I told you, I had my back turned. The next thing I heard was a scream, and I turned, and Dillon was bleeding from the neck. I don't know what Rupert was doing at this point, because I didn't look at him. I was focusing on Dillon, because the blood was just gushing everywhere.' She felt a small lump rising in her throat and a prickly feeling down her arms.

'I got some towels and pressed firmly on Dillon's neck. He'd collapsed to the floor at this point. It was then I noticed he was also bleeding on the face, but I didn't investigate to see if he had been stabbed twice. At this point I did look up at Rupert, who was green in the face –'

'Green?'

'Yes, he'd turned green. He ran away fairly quickly. Then John – Mr Keane – heard me screaming and he called the ambulance.'

'And did you find a weapon?'

'You mean the glass shard?'

'Where did the glass come from?'

'It was a flask that got smashed.'

'And how did it get smashed?'

'I don't know. Possibly before the accident – incident – happened. It may not have been a glass shard that caused the incident. But a blood-stained shard was found in the lab.'

'Didn't you hear it smash, Catherine?', he raised one eye-brow. 'Didn't you hear it?'

'I was writing on the board, I wasn't paying much attention. The first thing I heard was some arguing. Dillon was calling Rupert a chicken or something, then there was the scream.'

'Weren't paying attention! Clearly, the number one prerequisite is to always pay attention.' He leant forward on the desk.

'This was fairly clear cut' he began, 'The little Chinese boy attacked Dillon with a glass shard. Yes?'

'But I didn't see exactly what happened – and also Rupert mentioned Dillon had taken something from him. A photograph.'

'A photograph? Of what? What can be that important?'

'You would have to ask Rupert that, sir.'

'Basically, Wu smashed the glass. He stabbed Dillon with it in the neck. The neck! Possibly the eye! He ran off when he could see you needed help. What other explanation could you possibly need?'

'There may be an explanation,' she replied, a little breathless. A patch of red had spread over her chest and neck, as it often did when she was tense. Peter was an old man, a stubborn man. He'd put her on edge many times since she started working at the school, but this was something entirely different.

'I'll have to think clearly about it then, Peter.'

'Yes, you think about it, Catherine,' he replied. He scribbled violently at the corner of his notepad. 'The Wu boy has been with us for two years and I don't think I have ever heard him speak. Does he speak English?'

'I think he was born here. He's just nervous, that's all.'

'Boys like the Wu boy need to speak up a bit. He walks around the school like a little enigma, and people don't like it, Catherine. It can be odd, imagine how odd for a normal child like Dillon Jackson – '

His phone rang and he answered it on speakerphone.

'Yes?'

'Mr Wilson, the police are here.'

'Ok Glenda, one moment please.'

'Consider your answers carefully, please, before you talk to them. Don't forget, Catherine, sometimes what you don't know is as powerful as what you do.'

## Grace

Grace Wu used to tell her son that he had been carried over in her womb. That he'd had a cushy journey, floating in her amniotic fluid. That he'd been shielded from the wind and the rain. But, she insisted, he was 100 per cent Chinese. After all, he'd been conceived in his homeland. He was not a mistake. And even if he was, he was a good mistake: he was a boy.

She was 31 when she arrived in 1995. A late economic migrant. Her aunties, her uncles, had travelled this same journey decades before her, and under harsher conditions. Now they had restaurants, green and red monstrosities, and their children were university-educated. The grass was greener on this side they'd said. The cold, the taxes, the people; you could put up with anything because what mattered was the *yen*.

Grace didn't squeeze herself into the back of a lorry, nor had she clambered over rough terrains. She'd arrived on flight C-0319-HK from Hong Kong to London. She'd flown direct on Cathay Pacific, economy class, in an aisle seat by the toilets. She could remember how luxurious it felt; the air hostesses were dressed in green and had their faces painted in Shiseido. Up until her cataract operation, her eyes would still fizzle at the memory of being one of the first to touch that plane, to soil it with her greasy hands, to drop her orange peel under the seat in front of her.

When she arrived, she was picked up by Uncle Five, who owned a take-away. Uncle Five was the youngest. He migrated in the sixties. When his wife died of cancer, his grown-up children were unwilling to work in the take-away, suggested that he bring his niece over to do the work. The take-away was two steps down from Uncles Four and Three, who both owned restaurants and were just one down from Uncle Two, who had a small cash and carry. Uncle One had declared himself the first gay in the family three years ago and the family had little to do with him. He was just 'white noise', as they would say.

It was cold in England.

Uncle Five takes a sideways glance at Grace, still young and perky despite being a married woman for nine years, and says, 'My. Haven't you grown?' Grace is only 31. She is a married woman. For nine years now, she has been committed to a simple man who works as a cleaner in Hong Kong. He smokes and he gambles. They live with his family in a tiny apartment with two bedrooms. Both his parents are still alive. They keep asking when Grace will produce a grandchild. It's been nine years of trying and she hasn't been able to carry a foetus past eight weeks. When her body is tired, it expels the foreign object with a tight contraction and a pool of clotted blood. Thirteen times in nine years. Even if you aren't bored of trying, I am. Then she moved to England to make money – still a married woman, on paper at least.

Grace was given her new name by Uncle Two, because it would be easier to live with an English name than with a Chinese one. She lived above Uncle Five's take-away where she worked six days a week, serving chips, chicken fried rice and sweet and sour chicken to fat, pasty white people. They fascinated her; the women and men with yellow hair, so light that you couldn't see their eyelashes. No eyebrows. Glassy blue eyes. Dry skin, with brown freckles, their teeth yellowing and mismatched. She thought they ate better in England. Thought they lived better.

Her room was small. A group of students next door played loud music day and night. A cold draft would blow and retract through the window, taking the warmth with it. The walls smelt of chip fat. They smelt of sausage, of pies. They smelt of soy, they smelt of garlic. She smelt of garlic. It doesn't how many times you wash; you can't run away from what you've become.

About two months later, when she had started to learn the most basic words of the English language, she felt a familiar fullness in her stomach, a growth. She waited for it to pass, as it always did. But instead it grew. It grew and grew, until she couldn't ignore it any longer. She would have to tell Uncle Five. He would be angry. She would have to tell her husband, who would be surprised – very surprised. Her mother would be furious after they'd saved up for so long to raise the money for her Cathay Pacific ticket. Her in-laws would say stay. Leave the child in the room during the day. It won't die. But make some money first. Don't come home empty handed.

At first she worked without a whimper, without complaint. Her belly grew big and firm and people would guess what the sex; a son when it was high and firm – congratulations! A girl when it was low and round – never mind. When she was eight months' pregnant, her mother phoned. Told her there was no point coming home because her husband had got someone pregnant at work, and it was probably a son. This woman was walking around, belly full, demanding that Grace's husband got a divorce. But he wouldn't divorce, because Grace was still sending the money. She told her mother she wouldn't send another penny his way. She was staying in her garlic-scented box room in England with her Uncle who had busy hands. 'But you can't speak English', said her mother. 'My child will translate for me', she replied.

Rupert Wu was born on a warm summer evening. She was neither happy nor unhappy but hoped to give him the best possible future. To answer any questions of paternity, since neither her husband in China nor the man who had bedded her would see her, he gave her son a small picture of a handsome model cut out from the Chinese newspaper at the age of eight.

'Your father was a good man and has gone to make money for us. He will send it back to you and think of you all the time. Now don't ask me about it again.'

Now it was an English future for an English-born boy.

**Rupert**

His mother didn't understand. Not a single word he said. So he didn't say or feel anything in front of her.

It was the same routine. She'd talk to him in Chinese, loudly. He would mutter back in English, quietly. She'd ask him what he said in Chinese, even louder. He'd be forced to respond in Chinese to that she'd understand, hoping her vocal volume would match his soft tones, but she would always yell back, voice booming.

He lived above his great uncle's take-away. It had a grimy old counter, a kitchen and a storeroom downstairs, two bedrooms and a bathroom upstairs. His mother slept in the cold room on the left and he took the room on the right side that overlooked the back street where his thirteen-year-old possessions stayed. He had a television, a DVD player, he had Sky, a Playstation 3, a PC and the internet. Every inanimate item a boy could want.

On a Friday and Saturday evening he would go downstairs to help his mother in the shop. The rest of the week he would come home from school and sit at his computer. At 8pm his mother would call for him to go downstairs to eat dinner, which would often be rice, greens, some meat and a salty duck egg, then he would take a can of Coke from the fridge and return upstairs, with his mother shouting, 'Do your homework!' behind him. Then he would sit at his PC for the rest of the night. Occasionally he'd make a vague attempt at doing some of the homework before giving up and playing on the computer. He had over two hundred virtual friends; one in real life. Sometimes he forgot how to talk.

His friend in real life was called Ahmed. Ahmed was Pakistani and a Muslim. Ahmed's parents came to England back in the sixties, so he was third-generation British. He was a geek like Rupert, but he could talk, he had the confidence. Ahmed wasn't afraid to tell people at school to shut-the-fuck-up if he had to. *I have a right to be here too. My parents have been here forever. We pay our taxes. We probably pay more than you.*

Rupert was raised to keep his mouth shut. His mother said: *No matter how long you have been here, you will always be a foreigner. Stay quiet, don't tell lies and keep out of trouble. Sticks and stones may break your bones but names can never hurt you.*

He didn't try to make a white friend, and they didn't try with him. Since he would always be viewed as an outsider no matter what he did, he decided to slip through his schooling like a shadow. And so he was, until the incident.

She had noticed the mark on his left arm at dinner. It was a whitish scar next to a big, angry red burn. She had asked him what it was, where he had got it from, but Rupert didn't take his earphones out to answer. And he covered the painful scald with the soft sleeve of his jumper.

'Where did you do it? Have you been smoking?'

He took his earphones out. 'No Ma. Bunsen burner.'

'A what?'

'In science. A Bunsen bur – a lighter. For experimenting only.'

She frowned at him dubiously.

At one in the morning, after the chippy had shut, she tapped at his door.

'Son – are you asleep?'

'Yes.'

She walked into the room. The lights were turned off but his computer monitor burned brightly, the computer set on silent.

'Son, what is wrong?'

'Nuffin',' he muttered.

'Did someone hit you?'

He shook his head again, somewhat more hurriedly. 'No, Ma.'

'Son. I don't always have time to talk to you. You see I work every day. You see how hard it is sometimes for me.'

He nodded his head, his hand feeling sweaty from the pressure. He felt his heart pumping loudly, the blood swishing in his ears. He didn't want to be a liar – Hong Kong Buddhists said that in hell they would cut your tongue off for telling lies, but he didn't want to be trouble either.

'I have done the best that I can over these thirteen years but it hasn't been easy doing it on my own.'

He mustered a type of grunt, the only sound he had the strength to make.

'And now, I am getting old and I don't want much. I just want you to finish school and go to University. I want you to do something proper with your life, something that I could never do. You understand, don't you? Not for money but to do good.'

Rupert glared at his screen. Various windows flickered, calling for his attention but it was best not to move while his mother told him her lies.

'I stayed here to give you a better life. If you think I am hard, if I am unemotional, it is only to make you stronger.' She shook her head. 'But you say nothing. So I am lost. What do I do?'

He sat silently, his pupils remaining firmly fixed to the computer screen, his jaw clenching and unclenching. There were things he could say, things he wanted to say, but he knew once the words escaped everything good would have evaporated into the air. All she would see was what he had done wrong. If someone had hit him and he hit back, he would be wrong. If someone had stolen something and he told a teacher, he would be wrong. Anything that drew attention, anything that would inconvenience his mother would be wrong.

He knew the rules of being a good son. Taking up his mother's time was not a good-son thing to do.

Grace snapped suddenly; her back straightened, her voice was raised. 'You are useless. Completely useless. Useless son. Other people have sons and they are good. I have a son and I had a potato.' Her face was beginning to redden. She started to clench her jaw. 'So today, Son, someone from your school called the take-away phone. I didn't know what they were saying and your uncle wasn't here and the helper wasn't here. What could I do? I had to say double sorry. What did they want you for? Why do schools call parents, son? Only if there is trouble. Only if you have done something wrong.'

A boy of thirteen is too old to cry. He shouldn't have to cry ever again – maybe on the day his mother dies. But that was it. Afraid, he shrugged his shoulders tentatively. He was too nervous to turn his face to meet his mother's gaze, which was now unflinchingly stern. He swallowed firmly, and tilted his head slightly in her direction.

'It's ok Ma. I will sort it out.'

'Are you in trouble at school?'

'No, Ma. I will talk to my teacher tomorrow.'

'If you are in trouble at school I will kill you. I will. Did you do something wrong? Tell me the truth.'

He shook his head again, wondering where a thirteen-year-old boy could live without a penny to his name, where he could work. 'No. Not me.'

'Well good,' she began, 'you are an investment – do you know that? I didn't have you for nothing. I didn't raise you for nothing. I didn't come here to slave away for thirteen years for nothing. Do you think it's easy carrying a baby and working until the day you were born?'

'Sometimes I wish I wasn't born,' he blurted.

Grace said nothing. She walked towards him and with her knuckles, cast a blow across his face so hard that it knocked his glasses to the floor. The pain made his eyeballs ache. He sat still for a few moments. Then he bent over to reach for his glasses. He put them back on his face, and sat with his head dangling.

Grace left the room. He knew her hand must be smarting from the pain.

## Authority

People rarely knocked when the doors were shut and the board with the opening times were turned on its back. Sometimes it could be the deliveryman, bringing a parcel for the boy. A computer game or some gadget he had bought on his mother's debit card. Sometimes it was a joker, a child tapping on the door and running away, sometimes an adult doing the same thing.

The weather is mediocre as usual, not wet or dry; somewhere in-between. Like the city and its people, neither happy nor sad, without aim or direction. The take-away is closed at lunch. The fish man brings fish at 9.00. Today there is knocking on the front door at 11.00. Grace approaches it. Her jogging pants are covered in grey bobbled fuzz and her peach sweater is discoloured from being washed with blacks.

The policeman is like a tower. His face is stern and pale. He wears a fluorescent jacket and a hat. Next to him is a Chinese woman, perhaps someone who can translate.

The door is glass and the shop front is glass, so there is nowhere to hide. Grace hesitates for a moment. The policeman's chewing his bottom lip and she clutches the door handle for a second, reluctant to let him in. Finally she opens the door.

'Grace Wu?' he asks. She nods. She can recognise her own name. 'We need to talk to you about your son.'

# The Undertaker

*by Ovie Jobome*

———

IT WAS stormy when I set off that afternoon. And the Atlantic wind gathered pace, picking up greasy paper wrappers, jerry cans, black polythene bags, and flinging them along the dusty road outside. Hawkers and itinerant traders hurried past on their way home, their wares wrapped up securely, their hawking trays becoming makeshift umbrellas. The neighbourhood mothers snatched up their toddlers and strapped them to their backs, calling out to their other children playing in the compound to get inside while snapping clothes off the washing lines. Thick streaks of lightning divided the darkening sky. Crackling and shivering. The thunder rolled into our compound, rattling windows and making toddlers scream. It was raining ice. All across town the frozen chunks beat a staccato rhythm on the tin roofs. Kids slipped their mothers' grasp and dashed from their verandas to pick up pellets of ice, which they swiftly popped into their mouths before dashing back. Soon the ice became rain, pouring down as though from a giant tap. The air was infused with the scent of damp earth. The parched soil couldn't mop it all up, so the water gushed through the town, overwhelming gutters, and gathering flotsam which it hurled down the road and deposited in compounds. It ran eddies around Mum's timber-clad palmwine shed which stood near the compound's entrance.

We huddled on the veranda, and watched the rain do its thing. My thoughts were everywhere and nowhere. I missed my mum and my dad already. I wanted so much to reassure them. To hold their hand, gather them in my arms, protect them. To do, and be, all the things that I hadn't made happen. But now I was leaving them to an uncertain future, even though it contained the promise of betterment. Mum seemed lost in thought too, even as she stuffed another parcel of fried meat into my bag. Dad looked at me, glanced into the forest of raindrops, then looked at Mum as if to say *now it's just you and me. How are we going to cope…?* It was as though we had agreed that silence was the best way to express our fears and our sadness. And to silently nurse the hope that departure was just a stepping stone.

Undertaker arrived in the storm, his gleaming black BMW slicing through the rain and his windscreen wipers working furiously, spraying water this way and that. He honked his horn twice, and everyone in the nearby neighbourhood, all four compounds and families, craned their necks in our direction. Mum hugged me close. I let her warm tears bathe my cheek and my neck, and I tasted salt on my lips. She begged me to write as soon as possible. I promised not to let her down. Dad recited a prayer of protection over me, invoking St Christopher and pumping my hand vigorously.

'Go well, my boy.'

*Dad.*

'Know yourself, and remember we are waiting for your message in the next few days. Let us know how you are doing.'

'Be a good man, my son.'

*Mum.*

'Stay away from those long-nosed girls. And keep out of trouble … We'll be praying for you always.' Then our sobs took over.

Madian comforted Mum, then, with Undertaker honking impatiently, she flipped open Dad's giant blue-yellow-red striped umbrella, and gave me shelter all the way to the car, the wind and the unrelenting diagonal rain buffeting the brolly this way and that. I hugged Madian then slid into the car. I turned to wave at my huddled family, as Undertaker guided the car through the flooded compound and onto the street. The ditches were filled with muddy water and you couldn't tell where the road began or ended. I carried on waving. Many neighbours waved back. The last thing I saw in our compound was the pile of typewriters, stacked against the guava tree, holding their own against the rising waters. Goodbye ... Goodbye ... I kept waving, even though I couldn't see them anymore as the rear windows had misted up. Maybe it was my eyes.

'You can stop waving now.' Undertaker. Dark sunshades clamped over his eyes. 'They can't see you anymore.'

He concentrated on manouevring the car, sticking to the centre of where the road ought to have been, instinctively avoiding the invisible gutters. If you got stuck in one of those, a whole bunch of area boys would emerge before you knew it, offering to help you extract your car from the gutter for a sizeable fee. In fact, it's not out of place for some area boys to dig up ditches themselves then lie in wait.

'How much money have you got on you?' Undertaker said.

'About eight hundred dollars.' It was a miracle I managed to raise that money. Undertaker reckoned it should do, but he peeled a few notes from his dashiki pocket, and handed them to me, without taking his bloodshot eyes off the road. One hundred dollars. It continued to rain. Not extremely fat drops like before, but regular sized, the type that fall so slowly and languidly that you just know they are in no hurry to stop falling. The car windows were streaky and the mist on the windscreen kept coming back. Undertaker had to keep reaching for the yellow cloth in his glove compartment to wipe the windscreen from inside.

'Let's get things straight,' Undertaker began. 'You owe me five hundred thousand bucks.'

'I know that already, Rubber ...'

'Plus one hundred dollars. US.' He reminded me.

'As we discussed I'll start paying you back as soon as I get my hands on something to do ...'

'Listen to me.' He virtually snarled. 'This is a favour, so don't fuck with me ... Let me put it this way. I know your compound, your mother, your folks. Three months. Maximum. You get me?'

'I ... I get you, Rubber. As promised I'll ...'

'I don't take fake promises. You just do what has to be done.'

And that was that. We stayed mute till the Luxury Bus Motor Park, from which the 'luxury' buses picked up their passengers. It had grown dark by this time. I grabbed my bag from the back seat, collected the envelope of 'paperwork' from Undertaker, slid out of the car, and headed for the bus 'check in' area, leaping over puddles of flood water.

'Hey!' Undertaker called out to me through rolled-down windows.

'Hey.' I called back.

'Don't fuck up.' I suppose I had to take that as the sentimental side of Undertaker shining through.

'No problem.'

Then Undertaker rolled up his car window, did a splashy U-turn, and sprayed some arriving passengers as he hurtled away, oblivious to the torrent of curses.

It was an overnight stay at the Luxury Bus Motor Park ready for departure at the crack of dawn. I paid for my ticket and settled down for the night's vigil on a straw mat. I was one of the lucky ones. I had come in early, had a mat to myself and could pick my spot amid the glow of low wattage light bulbs. The walls were painted deep green at the bottom, and light green at the top. The ceiling was off-white. Sissal-bagged assorted goods were piled high in the corners. There were bags of rubber shoes and slippers, chilli pepper, plastic bottles, fabrics, potatoes. The ticket man shouted at a hapless passenger,

'Oga, we are not carrying tomatoes. And we are not carrying fish.'

'Why? What happens? I've been carry fish in bus many years. Young man please, let me hear word ...'

I hoped I'd be fast asleep by the time the other passengers arrived. Mosquitoes permitting. Mosquitoes never permitted. A cockroach zigzagged between my legs. I squashed it with my *No Longer at Ease*. If you gave them an inch they took a mile, the roaches. The smell of smoked fish in the newly arrived passenger's bags was guaranteed to keep the rats hopeful too. I opened my bag, unwrapped a bean cake Mum had packed for me and took out the paperwork. I took in what I could of the documents provided by Undertaker. The green one was my Nigerian passport, in my name. And a whole bunch of papers that I couldn't make sense of in French, and then Arabic. Undertaker had provided instructions of what to do with each one as I passed through Niger, Mali, Algeria and finally, Morocco. My heart lurched. Was this all a stupid pipedream? Was I just going to be running from pillar to post? So help me God, I prayed. I just hoped Undertaker knew his business.

The coach had become a crammed car where we sat and boiled. I craned my neck out of the car window to see if I could tell where I was, even which country I was in. But all I saw was the bright sun rising again, the heat already overwhelming.

Ibrahim had a serious-looking pistol under the driver's seat. He checked it constantly, warning of dissidents, bandits and undercover police. Hours blurred into days, or was it still only hours? My lips had stuck and unstuck so many times that they were chapped and sore. I tried to drizzle mucus down my throat to no avail. Then we entered pure desert and the most gruesome heat imaginable, a heat that irradiated my bones. I was squashed into the car with the others. And in that position, my legs swelled, my feet burst in my sandals. Then they went dead. I couldn't sleep but I couldn't stay awake. I fought for air, craved the slightest breeze, prayed for deliverance. But the journey rolled on and on till I was in a state of suspended animation. I dislocated body from soul a few millimetres at a time. But relief was always temporary.

Ibrahim left us in hills of Algeria. We festered in the slate and gravel hammada and waited. We ate couscous, bread, olives and dates. Violent winds licked the hammada clean, blasted our faces. Treacherous mountains beckoned from Western horizons. To the East, the bare desert sneered. We set off in the night again, with Hassan.

'Okay. Have you got all your passports?' he asked.

We all nodded yes.

'Give them to me.'

He tossed them all into a mud oven. It sent out an angry green plume.

'No other papers at all … any other papers?' He insisted we turned our pockets inside out. He took a list of UK-based names and phone numbers given to me by Undertaker and tossed it into the fire.

'Okay.' Hassan resumed. 'We're going through those mountains on foot. If all goes well, we can complete the journey in three days. Otherwise, we spend another day hidden in the mountains.' No papers, no provisions; just a small goat-hide flask of water for each person, worn on a shoulder string. And no bright clothes, or jewellery, and mines to avoid. Only three of us, and Hassan, made it through those mountains into Morocco. I barely made it myself. My fever was high, my mind hallucinating.

Now I could taste Europe in the air. My beard itched. My finger nails were black. Spots covered my face, my back, my legs. They pussed in places, sticking to my tunic. My mouth ached with ulcers, and my torn lips were too painful to lick. I felt light-headed, torn between exhilaration, starvation and dread of the crossing.

Hassan, bearded and armed, talked to us.

'While here, don't have anything to do with the authorities, not even the hospitals, or they will deport you back to the Algerian border and riddle you with bullets. So, low profiles.'

Bone-shrinking winds lashed at our tent, and the ocean roared through the night. Come daylight, the sun scorched us anew. Hassan wanted five hundred dollars for the crossing. He took it from me. He also wanted there to be at least twenty people on the trip for it to be worth his while. We waited for this, and the days passed. All I could do was stare at the Atlantic. I questioned myself. What foolishness was driving me on? The whole idea of making it big in Europe seemed like a juvenile misadventure. In my dreams that night my parents wore serious expressions, like they were dead, as if they already knew what fate would deal me. And in my unsettled and delirious sleep, Simbi mocked me. I told you so, her eyes reminded me. I told you you were a loser. Born a loser, ever a loser.

In the course of a few days, our camp swelled. People arrived from all over the continent, even a couple of Asian-looking guys, who spoke neither English nor French. Then one night, in the camp, Hassan told us we would leave very soon, the next evening if possible. In his own peculiar way, he sought to reassure us: 'You don't need to take anything with you. Not food, not papers. If you survive the journey, which you will *insha Allah*, Spanish patrol will be waiting for you with food and clothing, and hopefully papers. If you don't make it, God forbid, you still won't need anything.'

He explained the journey would take approximately a day, depending on the wind and the waves. We needed a full stomach when we set off, and a bottle of water each. We should not stand up in the boat, for if we did, it would capsize and we would die. Even when we saw the Spanish coastal patrol boats, we should remain seated till they were right upon us. And once rescued, or arrested, he advised, stick to your story. When telling them where you were from, you should stick to places where they'd seen suffering on TV: Rwanda, Sierra Leone, Sudan.

The next night it was time. Seventeen of us arranged ourselves carefully into the small boat, with a Senegalese captain. He was slight of frame, but cast a long shadow over us in the setting sun. The boat looked flimsy even to my untrained eye: new wood, unvarnished, with fresh tar lashings. Hassan declared it was built by the best boat makers around and ranked amongst one of the finest he'd ever seen.

We set off. With only a small motor for power, the waves flung us right out to sea, tossing out a man whose screams died in the waves. We held on to the boat, and when that failed we held on to each other, twined our legs. The brotherhood of the soon-to-die. The boat was flooded, but the boat hurtled on. In the froth, and amidst the rolling and the spinning, I had no idea which direction we were headed in, or how long we'd been travelling.

The sea played games with us. Now calm and easy, then rearing up at us, the waves tested our stamina, our ingenuity, all the while knowing its merest whim could completely overwhelm us. At nil visibility, with no monstrous wave to warn us, the boat hit something, fractured down the middle and tossed us all into the watery gloom. As I smacked the water, my head struck something hard and the world became tinged with yellow. The ocean scorned my screams, sucking at my limbs, submerging my lungs. This was it. I wished I could have been a better son, a better provider. *Goodbye Simbi*, I called, *I loved you once*. I cried for my mother too. All her suffering had been in vain.

Death, what are you waiting for?
> Why can I still feel?
> Why can I still hear the wind, the waves, taste the salt in my lungs?

… I was 6 years old. Walking through the woods, returning from school. Suddenly a naked woman stepped onto my path, from behind a big tree trunk. It was the first time I had seen an adult naked woman. She was mad. She had a thick growth of hair around her pubis and her breasts flapped as she closed in on me. I hadn't noticed her earlier, but now it was too late. The path through the woods was narrow, and the only way to avoid her was to step into the shrubs. So I stepped right into them. And she blocked me off. I stepped to the left, and she blocked my path again. My heart raced. I was convinced she was going to kill me. I started to run, ducking under her arms. She came after me and tripped me from the back. I ate undergrowth and mud. Then she stood over me, and started to whip my back with a twig. She accused me of truanting from school. But she was wrong. I knew she was killing me, so I screamed. I screamed for my mother.

'This one's alive…'
So this was what it was like to be dead. Other people still around. But how could the dead be conscious of their death? I was a spirit now. That had to be it. A spirit haunting the seas, and understanding new languages.
'Pienso que habla el Ingles. Ven aqui. Pronto.'
And the fact of my rescue began to dawn on me. I was in Europe.

'Don't worry, we will get you to Ukay', someone said above white sheets, 'Undertaker has left instructions. Sleep well.'

'What?' I exclaimed. But before my eyes could focus further, I felt a jab in my thigh and then the world tinged yellow once more.

# When Stories End

*by Martin De Mello*

---

**Prologue of a kind**

I arrive late and sit at the bar watching her performance in the mirror. It's unbearable. To look at her directly while she's on stage. In the mirror her edges are cool and defined, less dangerous than words.

*1.  Night may have known her*

I rarely went into jazz clubs. This one was full of smoke and the masculine drone of the audience. Some of them had come from the business district, others looked like factory workers who'd spent the early evening touring the bars near the railway station. I went to relieve myself and returned to a single light above the centre of the stage. Her heels made a slow, deliberate click. The drone stopped. She let the silence, standing there in the light. Until the band lost their nerve and began playing. I saw her voice in the smoke, her voice inhale and exhale. Her voice twisting through light towards darkness. This woman, I thought.

The shadow of her face, the shadow of her legs. I watched her voice, like the ancestors. Her voice in the darkness becoming separate from her. A voice akin to a star that has already gone, that has died and no-one yet knows. For two hours she sang. The band suddenly stopped. Johannesburg's night, smoke closing behind her.

*2. Train station, no longer works*

In films it is the hero and heroine that are centre stage at the train station. People like me are the extras. I stood near the entrance and watched the shop girls with their tired smiles after work. The tsotsi loitering by the stairwell. I avoided their gaze and turned my attention to the beggar with many stories about his one leg. He wore an old, shredded dustcoat and khaki pants. Where his leg was missing he had folded the khaki and tucked it in at his waist. His face and arms covered in sores

He'd collapsed drunk on the train track after the death of his son. He'd been involved in a feud with his uncle over a girl. His uncle had gone to a medicine man and paid them to give him bad luck.

–Hey, brazzo! Who do you think you are? Jolling in the way of my customers.

–Ah, what the fok! Cherries are all the same. Why lose your leg over one?

–Brazzo, my customers!

The 'customers' hurried past on their way to Soweto and Lenasia, the tsotsi casually following them. One or two of the girls threw him a few cents. He leered, showing his rotten teeth.

I grimaced. Through the noise and the smell, bodies in the heat and overcooked food bought at the stalls, I noticed the shadow of her legs shivering across the main concourse until they stopped at a man with merciful blond hair and a gun sticking out of his belt. Not Boer, he was Dutch, with that tall, languid cruelty. The cruelty only Europeans have. I felt a compulsion to confront him, to ignore his gun, to tell him that he and I and the townships live out our lives under the same sky. That we gaze at the same stars. And at that moment I wanted her. I wanted my gut pressed against hers. I wanted my arm slung round her waist. I wanted the feel of her hips and thighs. I wanted her skin. And to look her hard in the face and swear that the freedom our people were soon going to have would not ruin us.

A man should not cry. I learnt this from my mother. The woman who spent her days drinking. The woman who would chew on a curse with the bitter taste of lerotho, who sat in the doorway watching the shadows play silently between the huts. She would not say she was waiting for the man who'd abandoned her, who'd left his youth in the mines.

A man should not cry. I watched him, the Dutch man, the swagger he felt in his hips that this black woman, this African woman, this woman who had turned men into empty liquor bottles. The swagger he felt because this woman scat him with her arms. I wanted to swear. That Soweto, our struggle and the funerals. Instead I felt hatred. I felt it like mud drying on my skin. In a country where it was possible for someone held by the police to slip on a bar of soap and be fatally injured. The men I was with whistled under their breath at the volume of her curves. I hated them for not feeling my anger, for wanting her as a plaything for the night. As a liquor-dripped fuck. I hated them for not knowing how the ancestors spoke through her voice, for stabbing each other, for fucking a woman whether or not she opened her legs. I hated them and felt like I had fallen from the tenth floor, becoming aware of the starlings near the entrance flickering in the sky.

### 3. Words are words, the tune is just a tune

Desire has its patience, like revenge. I asked the stewardess as she passed how cold the air was at this height. Her reply robotic: minus sixty-seven degrees at an altitude of thirty-six thousand feet. Africa rippled below us.

I stood up from my seat and looked across the aisle. I don't remember exactly my thoughts. I was looking for a way to describe the continent I was leaving. Through the window there was a long sky and a short patch of brown. The dirt where consciousness and history began. Where humans first rose to fight the oppression of their environment.

I have heard it argued that what makes us human is our recognition of music. Baboons do not sing. Chimpanzees and gorillas don't invent musical instruments. The thought prompted me to retrieve my walkman and the tape I had brought with me from the overhead locker. The tape cool in my hand.

I knew it was her in the hand of the street seller, pushing a voice on a tape into cars by the traffic lights. The motorists waved him away and the traffic lights changed and grease dripped from the sky. He stood looking after them, wearing a bleached t-shirt and a baseball cap flipped round to cover the back of his neck. He had a wet-looking scar on his throat. I heard men singing in a truck on their way home and I thought of the words to a different song. A song I first heard in winter, when the dust had turned the roads and houses a dry red. We complained bitterly for rainfall. My mother's breath soured.

–Why you ask for the rain like so? When the first rains come the burrowing animals drown. Is it luck for us when it rains?

That plane journey was the first time I'd listened to the tape. Her voice filled the cabin with smoke. I thought of Newtown, like a beggar, the alleyways and backstreets leading to the club like beggars and thieves. Vegetables rotting by the side of the road. People crowding the pavements, smoking dagga, arguing when Madiba would be freed. Her face reflecting the single light, water reflecting the moon. The vibration from the trains as they shunted past. In her voice the gap between stars, the rift valley, our clenched fists, the sjambok and the necklace.

An enormous belly snored in the seat next to me. A hippo belly with skin like a whip. I didn't know what country he came from, what country he was going to. I didn't know myself if I would ever go back. If the distance was not greater than the distance an aeroplane could travel. I thought of the words to that winter song, knowing soon she would sing them:

The river come down / The river come down / River come down / I can't cross over / Why-o, why-o, why-o / I can't cross over?

## 4. Wounded without a shout

Ka Mkame amongst the shanties and the gangs, the hippos and the protestors, the mothers and the jails. *Letters to God*. His words are her words: my work is just what I see when I wake up in the morning. Ka Mkame knew his people.

Each morning I wake to rain. Rain that doesn't know how to end. What would Ka Mkame see on these mornings? Sfiso, what would you see in this old land not as old as ours? I see children of every age in equal numbers on their way to school, the youngest their mothers accompanying them. The old couple with their fishing rods on their way to catch trout. The white man who delivers letters and has never acknowledged me. I see red terrace houses, solid houses, and many cars parked on the road. And a slow, whining vehicle for the milk. I see the cheap cider drunkard returning with two blue plastic bags. A dog sniffing discarded chip papers. I see the photographs of her that I took; one next to my bed, the other on the wall.

The surprise trickled down her face, at the accent of a countryman. The cold air and wind hadn't been kind. Her skin was dry. I explained how well I knew her voice and where I'd first heard her. She told me she'd struggled to find work, that she could not tour the small towns. Her singing had changed. Bluesy was the word that she used, which seemed misplaced on her lips. A car passed, the radio blaring an electronic beat. She told me that she'd adapted her style and sung many songs at once with the same words, layer on layer with the same words. The song of her mother who had two husbands. The song of the old man who lay sprawled on the ground with his face in the dirt while she was raped. The song of her grandmother who never left Durban. The song of her grandfather who drowned crossing a river after the first heavy rainfall. The song of the unemployed workers who stood watching their homes being bulldozed. The song of the child that bled from her womb. The song of her people. Ka Mkame, you and she will meet when the world ends and you will work on only one picture, building your layer on layer of colour and same words, scraping away to find …

I was surprised to find that they have cockroaches here, jiving out of the kitchen, brave enough to examine your toes in the dark. And net curtains which are graveyards for flies. I was surprised when I met her, the miracle of her reincarnation. No longer the woman I'd first seen. She knew herself that she was out of place, a life-size mural painted on a side-street wall. I had my camera with me. While she stood I could see her voice smoke. But I am not good with a camera, my arm shakes.

It shakes at the elbow where it was broken. I told her my arm shakes and asked her permission. After three photographs she asked me why I came to this country? Not for work.

I have noticed that people here look at the sky as a kind of superstition. I looked at the sky when she asked me, at the blue wisps amongst the grey clouds. How had I come here, to a land of crocodiles? Is it possible to make any story into a song?

–That depends, my brother. We have songs for everyone back home, but *here* who is everyone?

The tone in her voice reminded. Of the way my heart stopped when the aeroplane landed. Of my pretence that my elbow didn't ache and that the sjambok scar didn't burn when the police detained me overnight. Their mouthfuls of spit were the rain.

I told her I pack shelves in a warehouse and that it's not such hard work as a clerk's office and does not ruin life like the mines. I told her and watched the blackness in my voice, even more black than at home. I watched my own voice disturb the litter rotting by the side of the road

–Brother, I have to go now. Maybe you will come watch me sing. Otherwise, I'll be seeing you walking after midnight.

## 5. Dark with perspiration

I had only just learnt there was a jazz club in town. Flipping through the *Evening News*, her name stuck in the corner of my eye. She was performing that Thursday. I swigged the rest of my coffee and went in search of the foreman. He was by one of the forklifts arguing with the driver. I waited for him to finish and took the opportunity, proposing an early end to my shift Thursday night if I made up the time at the weekend. He chewed on his pen and said he would think about it.

I arrived early on Thursday and found him hovering inside his office. Eventually he lost interest in his paperwork. His desk was well organised except for an ashtray with deformed cigarettes and his pen, which looked like a chewed straw.

–Right, you trying to look like a scarecrow?

–Remember, I talked to you on Tuesday. I need to leave two hours early.

–You're after leaving early now. In fact you *need* to leave early now. Your wife at the hospital is it?

–Sorry?

–So how many pallets are sat there waiting for yous?

–Seventeen. There's seventeen.

–Uh-huh. Seventeen. Now that's for you and the Paki. How long does one pallet take?

–One pallet … Twenty five minutes.

–And the Paki can do four pallets on his own in two hours?

–Ahmed's a good worker.

–God Almighty, I know he's a good worker, I didn't ask you if he's a good worker. That's why he's still employed at this establishment. The lad didn't even ask for time off when his mother was ill.

–His mother was in Bangladesh.

–Well then, my mother lives in Cork, his mother lives in Bangladesh, it's all the same difference. I've been waiting for the old woman to die since I was a snapper. Right now she's got a dicky heart and will only eat chips fried in dripping. The Pope himself has to pray to stop her from keeling over during Mass. So now what can be so important that you need two hours off?

–Not off, early. But the main thing is I will work the time at the weekend. Two hours extra at the end of my shift this weekend.

–Two hours, eh? Maybe while you're at it you can work the extra from all the times you've been late. The boss has been onto the timesheets. As a consequence it is my unpleasant duty to deduct three hours from you for last week.

I looked at his grey, cloudy eyes to try and determine his mood, if he was serious. His skin had bleached in patches and wasn't good. He drummed his fingers on the desk.

–If you're late that many times one more week don't bother to come back. The boss would step over ten naked women to get to a pint, he knows his own mind where his business is concerned. And sure as I'm here he doesn't like wogs, he only takes you on because you work hard. There'll be five more of you knocking at the door if you get fired.

His whites bloodshot and nicotine stained. The sensation of strangling him, spitting in his face. He's unable to read the look on my face or detect the singed flush on my cheeks.

–Why must you insult me in this way? What is it that I have done to you? I work hard, I don't stop every ten minutes for a cigarette like those English boys. I am late when my buses are late, I must catch three to get here. So what is it that you are saying to me?

I expected him to become angry. His body turned sideways and took on his agitation. He jabbed a yellowish finger.

–Eejit, get the feck out and make sure you give me the time owing next week. I don't employ you to come in here with your lip.

Everyone on the floor heard him, but his face didn't move. Only his voice and his mouth and his breath, which stank like a smoking room.

When I arrived at my house I got washed and changed, grabbed mealie bread and Umleqwa that was left over from the day previous, then stood at the bus stop wondering at the clouds. They seemed heavier and greyer and somehow out of place. By the time I reached town the air had become cold and dry. I sauntered through the streets kicking every stray bottle and drinks can, thinking Boer and Irish are the same, all white men are the same. I stopped twice to ask directions and stared up from the street at the red neon lettering wondering how I could get in. The door was clearly marked as a fire exit. I carried on down the road, turned left and left again, feeling my gut pain as if I had eaten bad food. An old man with a white beard bumped into a lamp-post and stood looking at the road. A girl emerged from one of the sex shops. She walked past and her perfume tasted like salted burnt almonds.I knew the entrance from the bouncer. The men here look different. He was big with muscle-packed shoulders and stood outside like a man who wasn't allowed in. We nodded at each other.

Entrance was two pounds so I could afford only one beer. I sat at the bar opposite a large mirror, drinking slowly and making my way through a box of cigarettes. I'm not sure if I expected the place to be full or empty. There were thirty-five or forty people in total, some of them having food. The lights dimmed and I felt my gut pain again as a man leapt on stage and introduced her. She noticed me as she walked past and made her way through the tables. A white man near the front looked directly at her and didn't clap.–Hey, brazzo, this one's a sweet cherry.

I heard the words inside my head, banging and thumping about. She introduced herself and I could hear myself softly curse. The woman on my right at the bar coughed and made her arm brush against mine. There were two musicians on stage, one playing the piano and the other a saxophone. She introduced her first song, an old song. I found myself alone in the bush and, one at a time, the stars in the night sky were becoming extinct.

I watched in the mirror. She looked at the man near the front while she sang. Her voice was no longer smoke. The man had blue, seeping eyes and her voice fluttered and hissed like a bad tape. His smile while she sang was a lump of sugar dissolving in tea. I tried to remember the hatred. Since the train station it had gone. I searched my pockets and found insults. In a land of crocodiles you must act like a crocodile. I lay on the bank in the sun, my jaws open. My tears were crocodile tears. She swayed and her curves swayed and I remembered that night. A room with eighty men all watching and listening to her, all toying with the idea of love.

She was beautiful. I watched the end of my cigarette, the smoke twisting as it fell into space, fraying like English hair. The song ended, her words faded out on the tape, I turned to the white woman next to me and we kissed.

Through the kiss I watched her song in the mirror. For one silvered note she let her gaze settle on mine. In that instant we were aware of each other, aware of who we had been that night in Johannesburg. And blackness like the night began snowing behind her.

*Note*

Sfiso Ka-Mkame is a self-taught artist, of Zanzibari descent, who was born in Clermont on the outskirts of Durban in 1963. He continues to live in the township of his birth and commutes to his studio in Umkhumbane/Cato Manor each work day. He obtained sporadic art training through the 1980s achieving an important success in 1988 with the sale, to the South African National Gallery in Cape Town, of his 'Letters to God' drawing series. He was an active United Democratic Front member and his early work reflected the political conflict, daily struggle and hardships he witnessed.

# The Container

*by Tariq Mehmood*

———

LADEN WITH human cargo, container M-61/t sat neatly stacked in a row of other containers. Seagulls floated noisily in the moist early evening air. Soon, very soon, these containers would be on their way from France, across the English Channel. Only then would this leg of the journey end for Javed Qureshi and the dozen other men, all strangers to each other, who had sat silently huddled together, in total darkness, in one corner of one of these boxes, vainly trying to keep warm. Almost eighteen months to the day when he had left England, Javed Quershi was on his way back again.

Three loud bangs against the outside of M-61/t signalled the start of the last leg of the journey. The darkness stiffened apprehensively as hands grabbed hands and backs pressed against cold metal walls, and the cold damp air, already pregnant with fearful sweat, became heavier to breathe.

Though his eyes were wide open, all Javed Qureshi could see were misshapen ghostly outlines of human figures of the men he had entered into the container with. Grainy darkness, bound together into a featureless form by an outline of reddish yellow light, slid effortlessly into a deeper darkness, a formless blackness, imprisoned by a chain of light that was shadowed by darkness. All floating aimlessly around in the darkness, bumping into each other, merging into each other only to slither out again. Somewhere, in the midst of the sound of heavy breathing, and occasional coughing of the men inside the container, were distant thoughts racing around trying to escape Javed Qureshi's mind and flash out in this darkness.

–The village drowning under a halo of mist.

–The lifeless black kicker tree.

–Strange smiles of his friends.

–The wedding. And the shame.

–Mocking eyes that followed him everywhere

–Javed's mother all flushed with happiness to have her son back in her arms.

–His sweet little sister, whose voice he used to long to hear. Too shamed to face the world.

–The rope still dangling off the branch and his sister's body turning round and round and round and round. Only moments earlier she had said to him, 'Elder brother, you should have spoken when they gave my hand to him. He was only interested in *abroadi* money and now I am done.' He had heard her words but had not listened to her. He had been buried under his own shame.

He had only left the house to bury his sister and then when he had come back home he had said to his mother, 'I have to go back to England.'

'This is not that son who I sent to England,' she had replied. Raising her hand she had asked of the Almighty, 'and what have you done with my son who I raised and whom I toiled to educate?' Turning to her son she had said, 'And you my son, unlike me are MA pass and you are all I have left now. God willing you will get a job, soon. We will not starve. And I have two other daughters and I will not let them die also. And you my son are all I have.'

'Give me your jewellery mother,' he had said, 'I have to go back to England.'

Something heavy crashed against the outside of container M61/t forcing it to shake violently. A deafening noised reverberated around the inside. This was not quite the sound Javed had been expecting from a forklift truck, which he had anticipated was going to move the container along. He had imagined the teeth of the forklift screeching down into the sides of the box, but this had been more like something had knocked against it. After a few moments of trying to visualise what going on, Javed concluded that it must be the crane putting its chain around the container. The container jerked violently before swinging from side to side. Some of the men's grips loosed as they flew across the arms and legs of other men. A box fell somewhere in the darkness and someone screamed for his mother in a language that Javed did not understand.

'Ssst now my friend,' a heavy African voice whispered. 'You are going to get us all caught.'

The man who had screamed cried out again. His voice was drowned out by sound of an engine roaring somewhere in the distance and the clanging and creaking of metal rubbing against metal as the container was lifted through the air towards the innards of the ship.

After a few moments the container settled down with a loud bang that ricocheted around the walls in the blackness. A metal chain was unhooked from the top.

'When I get to England, I am going straight to a mosque and praying,' a crisp youthful voice shouted out from somewhere in the lightless room.

'Be quiet now, son,' an elderly voice interrupted, 'we are to no talking. Yes!'

'Even God can't hear us from this hell,' the youthful voice laughed. 'And I have done that since I was a kid.'

'All money I have, I have paid for getting to England. Now please you keep quiet,' the elderly voice said.

'You can talk as much as you like now friend,' Javed said, brushing something wet and warm from his forehead. A sharp throbbing pain began to rip through his head. Javed tasted the wet substance. It was blood. Pressing onto where he thought the cut was, Javed said, 'You can talk or you can shout. There is no one to hear you now.'

'Help me, Jaanilaal, help me,' the man who had earlier screamed shouted meekly.

'Just hold on, elder brother,' Jaanilaal replied, 'I coming to you.'

'How long before we get to England?' Yousaf asked over the groans of the injured man. 'Does anyone know?'

'Not long and too long.'

'Who said that?'

'Does it matter?'

'In God's name, Jaanilaal, where are you?'

'Here, here elder brother,' Jaanilaal said, 'I'm here. Here, drink some water.' Then Jaanilaal shouted loudly into the darkness, 'My brother needs some help. He has damaged his leg.'

'There is no help for him here, my friend,' said Javed.

'He is bleeding very badly.'

No one replied.

'I am not going to let my brother die.'

'It is so cold in here we are all going to die,' someone said.

After a brief pause Jaanilaal starting bashing his hands against the sides of the container, shouting 'Help' all the time.

'Can someone give me something to knock against the wall?'

No one replied.

'This will do,' Jaanilaal said to himself as he began to bang some metallic object against the sides of the container.

'For God's sake, stop it now,' someone shouted angrily above Jaanilaal's knocking.

'You don't want this container's door opened till we have crossed Dover,' Javed warned.

Jaanilaal continued on with the banging and shouting for help. An eternity seamed to pass when Javed heard a different sound bouncing off the walls of the darkness. Someone was knocking from the outside.

'God help us now,' Javed said.

The door of the container suddenly swung open. The men inside turned their heads quickly away from the blinding light, which suddenly exploded into the darkness. Droplets of rain rushed in on gusts of sea air.

Javed Qureshi's body stiffened in terror as he tried to focus his eyes on the figures silhouetted in the entrance. A small round man was standing in between two much taller ones. The small man moved forward a little, inhaled on a thick cigar and held the smoke inside before breathing out again. The smoke spiralled upwards in the shaft of light that was tearing into the container. The small man cleared his throat and said, 'I am captain. We tell you no noise.'

'I am hurt very badly sir,' the injured man said whilst squinting his thick brown eyes.

The captain stepped inside the container, looked across at the injured man, shouted something across towards the ship-hands standing at the entrance, smoked on his cigar and calmly walked out of the container. The ship-hands quickly moved into the container, grabbed hold of the injured man and dragged him outside. Jaanilaal was about to stand up when Javed pressed tightly onto his hand and stopped him.

The captain stopped by the entrance, turned around and ordered, 'no more noise.'

As soon as the captain was out of the container, the doors were slammed shut again, imprisoning the men into darkness once again, but this time, it was resounding with fear.

'Were these English men?' the youthful voice asked.

'They were Eastern European,' Javed replied.

'Which country?' the youth asked.

'I don't know.'

'They were Ukrainian,' the African voice said.

'How do you know that, brother?' someone asked.

'I have worked there.'

'Well, at least they will sort my brother out.'

'That is not what they said.'

'What did they say?' Jaanilaal asked fearfully.

There was no reply.

Perhaps it was the motion of the ship labouring over a rough sea that had rocked Javed into a kind sleep. Or maybe it was the dance of the macabre shapes floating in the darkness, just above where Jaanilaal's brother had lain groaning that had taken him out of this darkened consciousness. He was in a world that seemed like a dream. A world in which he felt conscious of his own being. He was looking at himself, staring over his own shoulder, at his mother, whose distraught face gleamed silently on, gazing at him, through him, past the taxi which had come to collect him, and dissolved deep into the dark brown rugged hills in the distance. She had just said,

–You don't have to go, son. God will provide for us.

The hills echoed back, –God will provide for us.

Parrots from the ancient peepal tree, which had shaded his childhood went eerily silent.

The door of the taxi swung open.

Javed's mother's tears fell loudly to the ground.

Startled parrots flew noisily out of the tree and hovered over Javed's head. The sky rained heat.

–At least tell me why you must go back to the white man's cursed land.

The hills hissed back, –That cursed land.

–I have to regain something, Mother. Something I have lost.

–There is nothing that we need which we cannot buy here.

–It is not something that can be bought.

–I need nothing but you.

–I am now nothing without it.

–What is that which my son seeks so much that he can leave a grieving mother?

He lowered his eyes in shame.

–Lift up your head, my son.

–I cannot.

Javed's mother was hugging him. He smelt her strong sweat and remembered the days when she used to take him into the fields where she had cut grass for the animals.

Javed snatched himself free off his mother's embrace and got into the taxi. His mother slapped the hot roof of the car with her open palms.

The hills echoed the cries of the mother's slapping. The banging got louder and louder as the car pulled away from under the shade of the peepal tree and raced towards a long dark tunnel. It was cold inside the tunnel. He tried to block the sound of the noise with his hands. The pain became unbearable and he screamed.

'Who was that?' a couple of voices asked in unison.

Javed Qureshi opened his eyes. There was a pungent smell of urine mixed with the heavy musky smell of the imprisoned stale air. A bitter chill gnawed into his bones. For a moment he half expected to see himself coming out of the tunnel, but then the monotonous roaring darkness brought him back full to consciousness.

Javed Qureshi smiled to himself as realised that he had been dreaming about the noise, but something was knocking against the outside of the container. It was as though someone was dragging a metal bar along side of the container. The rattling noise started at one end of the container and slowly passed over Javed's head and continued on towards the door where it stopped.

'Are we in England,' someone asked excitedly.

'We are still at sea.'

'I think we have stopped.'

'This ship is still moving ...'

The doors of the container suddenly crashed open. The beam of a powerful searchlight captured the men in its merciless glow. Javed Qureshi turned his head away from the light but it bounced off the back wall, cut through his hand with which he was trying to protect his eyes and burnt itself into his mind. A ripping pain rushed through his already aching head. Javed slowly turned his head towards the light. All the men were huddled together. An engine of some sort roared close to the source of the light.

'Get up and get ready,' the captain ordered as he stepped into the light. His shadow stretched across the container and covered all the men.

Looking out of container, Javed realised that it was still dark.

'Get up and get ready,' The captain repeated himself coldly.

The men stood up and moved into the shade of the captain's shadow.

The tall strongly built dark-skinned Jaanilaal walked nervously towards the captain and asked, 'How is my brother, sir?'

The captain stepped out of the light and walked out of the container. Jaanilaal turned his head away from the light.

'Pick up all of your things,' the captain said firmly from the shadows.

'Where is my brother?' Jaanilaal asked softly, rubbing his blood-shot eyes.

Four tall uniformed men, carrying long metal bars, stepped out of the shadows and walked into the container. Two more uniformed men, carrying automatic weapons, stepped in after them.

'I just want to know about my brother,' Jaanilaal said apologetically stepping backwards.

One of the uniformed men took a few quick steps towards Jaanilaal and struck him violently across the head. Jaanilaal screamed and then dropped to the ground. Two of the uniformed men grabbed Jaanilaal by the legs and dragged him out of the container. One of the doors was now slammed shut but the other was left slightly ajar, that filled the interior with a soft grainy light that bounced off the walls.

Before Javed and the other men had had the time to come to terms with what had just happened more uniformed men came entered the container. Javed felt a large rough hand tightening its grip around his arm. He felt a jerk and then found himself being pushed into a line of men that stretched towards the entrance of the container.

'What is going on, mate?' Javed asked the man who had just pushed him into the line.

The man looked ahead and pretended not to hear. His long thick reddish- brown moustache twitched nervously.

'At least tell us what is happening, mate,' Javed asked again.

The man brushed his moustache, waited for a few moments and then quickly whispered to Javed, 'The English coastguard may be boarding this ship.'

The door of the container opened fully a moment later and Javed saw Younas being frog-marched out.

'Are we going back to France?' Javed asked as the door was brought back to its earlier position. The guard looked stiffly forward.

The door opened again and another man was marched out. There was a long pause before the door opened again. The ship-hand guarding Javed moved closer to Javed who noticed he was struggling to hold back tears.

'I am so sorry,' the ship-hand said with a quivering lip.

# The Salesman Saleem

*by Matthew Curry*

B EHIND THE Pennines the sun had just come up. There was now some light mixed with the dark in Bolton. There was a knock at the bedroom door.

'Father, it is time to wake up.'

Saleem lifted his head. He flicked the bedside light on and looked briefly at himself in the fitted wardrobe's floor-to-ceiling mirror. Black hair with a grey streak – he must dye it again soon. Face a young forty. But he feels older than forty sounds.

'Father, today you are going to get a big sale'

'Yes, son. I am.'

Saleem Junjena had not made a sale for nearly two months. He was superstitious and had not changed his shirt for this period. He reached across to the wardrobe and slid the door from his image. No-one noticed it was the same shirt. It was pure white cotton like all his others, and he was a man who didn't sweat.

'You know, Mohamed, I love the people I sell to, you know that, don't you?' he said.

'Yes'

'The new breed, the cynics, they despise customers, they are like hyenas, getting revenge for the hurts they have endured: insults, rejections, all that.'

'You are like a lion, father.'

'Yes I am, son. Yes I am. I respect the people I do business with. I draw the sale from them, I do not impose it. I don't bombard or bamboozle. By the end, although I cannot see them, I know there is complicity on their faces. Even if they have been a bit naughty, pushed the boat out, they are glad of it. I only do it ...'

'… if you identify a genuine and otherwise insurmountable need.'

'Exactly son, you understand. What can we muster for breakfast? We should be fasting – but you are young still and I am reluctant. As you said earlier, the day … today is auspicious.'

'Remember that time you were without a sale for forty-eight days. And then the twenty k?'

'I need a bigger one now. If things don't improve they'll not keep me on much longer. And then where will we be? We'll be in Dickie's meadow, that's where.'

'Remember all you've been through, Father.'

'Yes, this isn't Uganda, sunshine, ha-ha. I was about your age when we left, but you know all this I must have told you …'

'I like to hear it, Father.'

'And expect me late.'

'I know, Father, snooker to celebrate.'

'Yes, I'm going to go far out today; the unlikely ones won't have been targeted before. Not the old, the rich, the old loans. I dreamt about it last night, like the depths of the ocean, a really big one no-one else would see, no-one else would look for, just a balance, a waver in the voice, a cry for help, I will be all tendril for it.'

'I believe you will, father. And they will be glad.'

'The one who can't ask, can't bring himself to even put out the normal signals, a traditional Englishman. In this new generation they don't exist. They're all little Americans now. Not you though.'

'Not me sir, no sir, no.' Mohamed salutes American style, short way up, and down.

'Hope Wogan's on this week. He gets me in the right frame. He's got the right take, the old charm.'

'What did you think when you first saw Bolton, father?'

'I've told you before. Shit heap. Pardon the language. And I didn't think it in that expression of course. I don't know. I think it was just vague disappointment but relief, huge relief at the same time. This land, my saviour. Which is why I love that sea of people. Not always in every circumstance but generally. And why they don't. The young sellers. With their Red Bull, hyperactive go-get. Because they know nothing. Nothing but porn and sick jokes and hatred. But it's not their fault. But it would be yours because you know better.'

'Yes. Dad. Don't have too many Guinness tonight and drive.'

'Ok, son, ok. I'll bring my tinnies home. You won't grow up and drink, son.'

'No.'

'That'll make your mother happy. Wherever she is.'

Mohamed went and got his father's pen from the bureau, then fetched his leather jacket from the hook in the hall and laid it across the bottom of the banister. He took a plastic microwavable box full of long-stewed mild lamb curry out of the fridge in the kitchen, put it in a blank white carrier bag, wrapped that round and round and put it into his father's shoulder bag. He reboiled the kettle and filled up his father's coffee flask. He also made him a small strong black coffee to drink now.

Saleem took a few sips, thanking his son and remarking on how it was just right, before going back upstairs to relieve his bowels. Each task must go right and in order, to feel right upon arrival at the blue glass towers. Even the men manning the barriers at the multi-storey car park must get the right message. Comfortable with himself, no neediness, no cockiness. Relaxed.

There were no tools he needed to gather, to check, to take with him down the A666, then the M60, which would be a long slow slog. Only himself. The LCD screen, the mouse and the headset waited for him. Two months. He knew, and Mohamed knew, that the young salespeople all regarded him as finished, an old legend who had become jinxed. A Jonah. He knew the smirks, the asides, he'd seen them directed at others. And now he dismissed all that from his mind.

Saleem descended the stairs slowly, his eyes steady and far off.

'You're already at work, aren't you, Father?'

'Ha-ha. Yes, son, I suppose I was, yes.'

It was a thick and throaty laugh Saleem had; earthy, dirty even, but benign. A kind of divine amusement. His dark and liquid eyes became more visible. He put out his soft warm hand, whose skin had never seen manual work, an Oxford don's hand, and patted his son's head; the hair just like his had once been, crow black.

'You'll get yourself off to school on time ...'

'Of course.'

'And lock up properly ...'

He walked into the kitchen and looked into the small yard. Checked the back door that he had checked last night before going to bed. Checked the spare key in the box on the side. Checked the oven was off, as he had done the night before. Checked that the heating was off. Checked the window lock. Then went back out to where his son was waiting, now holding his leather jacket. He took it from him, picked up his bag and left, the knocker knocking straight after the door shut. By the time the red N-reg Carina pulled away, Mohamed was on the phone.

'Be round in ten minutes. Yeah, skin one up. Can't face double science straight. My dad's just been doing his double checking. Does my head in. He's cracking up ... Innabit ...'

Mohamed pressed the red button on the cordless phone. To his friends he maintained this idea of his father as a pitiful failure, a neurotic has-been. It was a way to displace, to project out.

In the slow queue on the inside lane of the M60, from which he'd come off onto the M602, Saleem could no longer hear Terry Wogan or the music in between. He had gone off to his dream place: he was a child in Uganda, sitting and watching and still marvelling at the huge white television his father had managed to acquire.

A faint smile on his face, changing gear without noticing, second to third, behind him loads of faces peering in through the window. Little barefoot black faces gathered at the window to gawp at this strange machine.

Saleem knew this recurring daydream displaced him again, from

Bolton and Manchester, from his son at his desk at the good school. Perhaps he had become addicted to displacement, he thought. Perhaps it defines him.

\* \* \*

At each circular desk there were four people, headsets on, each talking and concentrating on an LCD monitor, flicking into and out of different screens, their forefingers on a mouse.

Saleem logged on to the system then logged on to his tally, which brought up the sales hooks prompts, the performance tool, the schedule tool. Saleem clicked the red cross to a green tick and waited for the yellow bar and the beep which meant a call was there.

On this floor were maybe fifty desks, so that at peak times, when they were all full, the noise generated was loud, like the old mills must have been, Saleem thought. Where his mum worked after they came here. The constant noise disorientating, harsh; not at all like pub noise. And the louder it was, the louder Saleem himself had to talk and think, to hear himself. He hadn't had loud thoughts before he worked there. And he had to listen so much more closely and intensely to the voice on the phone, to try to block out everything else. In the mills one would have been silent. Here, the fluorescent lights, hard blue carpet tiles, big windows and blinds; the yellow sofas in chill-out areas. These are the information mills, he thought.

'Good morning, thank you for calling, how may I help you?'

'I hope you can. But I very much doubt it.'

'Well, let's see ...'

Saleem is already whizzing through screens of this customer's details ... what he could sell the guy, what he's good for, account activity, history, product holdings.

'I paid a large cheque in last week and I can't use my card – won't take it – I've had enough of this bloody bank ...'

'I can see that as a credit entry, yes. Thursday. It's not due to clear 'til this Wednesday.'

'That's a bloody disgrace. Where's the interest go?'

'Did you not know it took five days, sir?'

'Three days I was told.'

'Never been three days sir. Let's look and see if there's any problem with the card itself.'

'I want to know where my money is.'

'Well, it takes ...'

'But who's got it?'

'Let me go through to ...'

'Look, I can't even buy cigarettes, I've ninety grand paid in last week.'

'If you'll let me, I'll try and sort out what the problem is by talking to debit card services.'

'I'm going to move all my money out of this bloody bank, I've had enough. These bloody call centres. I bet you're in bloody Bombay, aren't you? You don't sound English.'

'Mumbai'

'Where's Mumbai?'

'I'm not in Mumbai, I'm in Manchester. Mumbai is the correct name for Bombay.'

'You what?'

'I'm in Manchester, sir. Can I go through to find out about your card now?'

'Who's got the bloody money, that's what I want to know. It's a con, the whole bloody thing.'

Saleem cut the customer off, put his computer into walkaway mode, took his headset off, stood up and walked to the drink vending machine. Twenty pence piece, number seventy-six, wait for the beep. Save his flask of decent coffee for later. Beep and yellow band when a call comes in. Beep when a drink's ready. Beep, well a bell, when the lift arrives and a voice tells you 'Second floor, doors opening'.

Saleem can already feel the looks through the window behind him, the little black faces. He's taken one call, it's only ten past nine.

He drifts, alert but passive. Saving himself. He mustn't care. It's all about self-deception. Staving off desperation. Is that what he's lost over the years, the real power of self-deception one has in youth, that women find so attractive, because it makes you easy to manipulate? But now he is weak and unfoolable. No wonder he gets nowhere with women anymore. And if he's honest he doesn't really want to. They bore him. Is it the same with sales? He doesn't really want the sale like he used to, even though he's more desperately in need. He sold laptops and PCs when they cost a fortune. He was the best then. Could just about switch one on but knew he was on fire. Knew from just the way they stood they were going to buy. On the phones it's more sly. More like fishing. Selling laptops was a lion on the savannah. This is fly-fishing. One needs delicacy and finesse. Not that he had ever been fly-fishing. Fancy a Ugandan Asian fishing on the Ribble say. Maybe he should, he'd laugh at that himself. Time to move on. These call centres of the north, they'll be gone soon. Bound to. Mumbai, Chennai, all over.

\* \* \*

'Eight.'

A red and a black and he is already out of position. All day again with nothing. Not even close. Difficult red to cut along the bottom cushion. Safety or the pot. The pot. Maybe blue then.

The red stops in the jaws, and Askhar grins.

''Sup, Sal? I'd've put money on you for that one normally.'

'Still thinking about safety on the pot.'

'You're not the man you were, Sal.'

'Don't I know it. I'm still twice you, Askhar, though eh? Let's see what you can do, ha-ha.'

\* \* \*

Saleem increased the Toyota's speed to ninety. The motorway isn't busy. Most of the time he'd been on the inside lane. The odd lorry, van, slow car. He unclipped his seatbelt. Askhar will take him in, surely. He wasn't sure, but it wasn't enough to stop him. He coughed a little dry cough. Ninety-five now, ninety-six. He concentrated on numbers.

Maybe the engine will blow. He never goes this fast. As the next concrete bridge approached, Saleem became calmer, looked in his mirror for the little faces. He steered slowly off towards the base of the bridge, nothing too sudden. He heard his father's voice above the television. There in the concrete was the face of his wife in the delivery suite, and a glimpse, annoying, of the fabric of the chair he was sitting on in the hospital; a rough green fabric.

# English Babu

*by Vijay Medtia*

———

OUR SECOND son is causing us trouble. He wants to marry an English girl. Anita has been crying for days thinking about the humiliation this will cause here and back in India. She blames herself for failing to bring him up 'properly'. Though what she had in mind for 'proper', I'm not sure. A decision has to be made soon. He'll be bringing Rebecca to the house at seven tonight. Either we bless the union or we lose our son. He's stubborn and in love; he'll go ahead and marry the girl. I don't know why we should feel so surprised. Wasn't this inevitable? I've lost count of the friends who've gone through the same nightmare. Isn't this the price of coming to England?

My father gave me three pieces of advice when I first left for Manchester in the autumn of 1965. Work hard; stay for five years only; return to India or you'll regret it. Well, five years have become forty. Forty years is a long time by any standards, but at times like this, it feels even longer. I came to England full of youth and vigour. I thought five years was all I needed to strike it rich. But when the five years had passed and nothing out of the ordinary had been achieved, it dawned on me that this England enterprise might not be so easy.

The first house I rented was pretty much the same as any other. A row of houses facing other similar houses across the cobblestones, their red bricks darkened with age and soot. Short stubby chimneys rising out of slated roofs, throwing out dark smoke into grey skies. The rooms were barely furnished and the walls covered with old patterned paper. Most rooms had no carpets. It was cold, damp and miserable; when I wasn't freezing, I was shivering. And there was the constant threat of a runny nose or being struck down by flu. I wonder now how I survived those cold winters with nothing but old blankets and hot water bottles.

I came from a prosperous family in the north of India and I graduated in Commerce. My high hopes of finding a good job over here were met with one rejection after another. Finally I found work in a mill in a corner of north Manchester; fixing valves on an industrial machine became the main stay of my early days and income. But it was a job and I was grateful. Recently, whenever I'm feeling stressed, I seem to drift back to them days. They were difficult times for sure but there was something innocent about that time too.

Certain memories stand out from them early years; the heavy snowfalls, the chimney smoke and cobbled streets lit by old gas lamps. These things seem like a distant memory now. Where's the snow now? And who'd heard of global warming then? There was the mania for the Beatles, black and white television with hardly any channels, and that first landing on the moon.

When I returned to India, the villagers said I was telling 'fairy tales'. They'd heard some things on the radio but they refused to believe it. 'How can man go to the moon?' they asked. 'How can man go so far? Going to England Ramesh telling many lies!'

I laughed but what was the use? They would never believe it. Most of them hadn't even travelled to Bombay. An old aunt once pulled me to the side and asked quietly, 'Ramesh, tell me. You will fly to England yes? How the plane stays in the sky for so long without falling?

'Magic,' I said. 'All magic.'

That word has some resonance. Considering my former life, my times in England have been like a magic show.

Anita joined me a year later when I had managed a little saving and moved to a bigger house. She hated England from day one; the cold damp climate, the strange white faces and, above all, the loneliness. The loneliness kills you for sure. It was the same for all of us migrating to a cold new world. The place was at work on me without me realising it, spreading its tentacles right to the tips of my fingers. My brown skin looked more or less the same, but day by day the old conservative customs were giving way to more and more liberal beliefs. The change expressed itself in the most unexpected sentences.

When we returned to India with our first-born son, I said quite casually one afternoon, 'How polluted everything seems? No cleanliness and why is there no road traffic sense? And by God it's so hot here.'

Father had laughed and looked out across the wide green fields, saying, 'Our Ramesh has become an English babu.'

'I haven't become English,' I replied, irritated.

'Oh yes you have. And, by the way, it has already been six years in that foreign land. When are you returning home?'

'Father I can't. I'm finally making progress and I'm buying my first house. My son's got a British passport. I need to make some good money before I return.'

He had laughed again, this time shaking his head as well.

'That is what they all say. You will not return.'

Anita still hadn't quite come to terms with England, but change was at work here as well. Her first trip back to India had also opened her eyes; her sisters and brothers were clamouring to come to England. They envied her lifestyle: the international flights, the cars, the pounds. And when she protested that it was a lonely and miserable existence, they dismissed this as a small inconvenience.

In the next few years we had another son and a daughter. The house was full and there was little time for boredom or loneliness. The first house I owned was a terrace, but from that moment I felt more secure than I had previously. So Anita too started to settle and make friends. The loneliness eased.

Even back then I knew several Asian men with English girlfriends. When we met in the smoke-filled pubs they always said, 'These English women are so beautiful.'

I met one of the English girlfriends of my friend once. His name was Haribhajan [meaning songs to the Lord] but she shortened it to Harry! Even the local regulars had labelled her a 'bloody tart'. But to Harry, she was the most beautiful woman he had ever met. He was a Sikh, but had removed his turban and his beard, and with it his bearings and his roots. She gave me the eye when Harry went to buy a round of drinks at the bar.

'You look a bit posh,' she said.

'I'm not.'

'I bet you are, and bloody loaded as well. If you ever need to go out for a drink ...'

'I'm married.'

'Oh don't let that stop you,' she leered and squeezed my thigh.

'I'll keep it in mind.'

'You make me go all tingly all over,' she said, shaking her ample breasts. And you can speak the proper Queen's English you can, unlike Harry, bless him. He can hardly stitch two bleedin' sentences together.'

He can't speak proper English, I thought.

Harry returned with two pints of lager and said, 'Isn't she wonderful, Ramesh?'

'She's wonderful all right,' I said.

After they married she remained true to her label and took him to the cleaners.

Of course because of my education and improving English, I met men and women who were gentle in manners, kind and considerate. I had also been made Supervising Manager. It was steady progress, but not quite how I had first imagined my life in England. On the whole, I've formed this opinion of the English: they're a good-looking race with a good sense of humour, integrity and fair play. Racism is there in some quarters, but Indians are guilty of this too, even in India. Who can stand on the moral high ground anymore? Every superior group or class looks down on the one below it, and even finds amusement at their expense. This is found everywhere in the world.

The time has come however. It's a little past seven, and there's a knock on the door. Prakash escorts Rebecca into the living room. The family greets them with much awkwardness. Mother sits to my right, adjusting her light coloured sari and round glasses. Sanjay, my eldest son, sits next to Anita on the main sofa and stares at the floor. He has avoided eye contact with everyone.

Rebecca passes a bundle of flowers to Anita with a smile. Anita I can tell is in a state, she is unsure how to handle this situation, and she sits down slowly. But Rebecca isn't how we expected her to be. She's wearing a floral blue summer dress, and her dark brown hair bounces past her shoulders. She's quick to smile, and the smile is warm and welcoming. For all his faults, Prakash has picked a beautiful girl. The silence grows, however, and the only sound comes from the clock on the mantel piece.

'I've heard so much about you,' said Rebecca, turning to Anita, and then to me.

'I'm sure he has plenty to say,' I reply.

'It's all nice things.'

'Where do you live, Rebecca?'

'I live with my parents in Sale.'

'Have they met Prakash?'

'Yes, lots of times. They like him very much.' She turns to look at him, squeezing his hand tight.

'What do you do?'

'I'm an assistant sales manager at Debenhams.'

'That's very good.'

'Tea, would you like some tea?' asks Anita, rising from her seat.

'I'm fine; please don't go to any trouble on my behalf.'

Anita sits down again unsure how to act. If this had been an Indian girl with relatives, so much fuss would have been made. Tea and snacks would have been served without any objection. Anita looks at me to keep the conversation going. Sanjay still hasn't looked at Prakash, and I don't like it.

'She's a very pretty girl,' says Mother all of a sudden. 'Too pretty for our Prakash, and too good.' She stares at Rebecca with a slight smile.

'Now Grandma, we'll be sending you to a Home if you don't behave,' said Prakash.

'He's so rude, why do you bother with him?' she fires back.

'I like him very much, Grandma, that's why,' replies Rebecca with a smile.

'Rebecca dear, do you like a roast?

'Oh yes, very much.'

'Beef roast, do you like beef roast?'

'Mother, there is no need for that,' I intervene.

'I'm trying to become a vegetarian,' said Rebecca unconvincingly.

'I'm not going to stop her from eating beef,' said Prakash, raising the stakes. 'I mean it's just an animal, like all others.'

'To us Hindus, it's a sacred animal,' said Sanjay. 'We consider her as one of our mothers, for we consumed her milk whilst we were infants. But I don't expect you to understand all these things, Prakash.'

'I understand plenty, brother. You can eat as much as you like, darling,' replied Prakash, 'I don't mind. Father we're getting married in October.'

There was complete silence again, so he added, 'I know you're not keen on the idea, but one day you will all come around. I love Rebecca very much, and she loves me.'

Then he stared at Sanjay and asked, 'Why don't you say what's really bothering you, brother?'

'What's left to say Prakash? You only make announcements.'

'Boys, don't argue in front of our guest,' I said.

'I think there is a need, father. I need to know to where you all stand,' said Prakash.

'Rebecca is a lovely girl, a credit to her family...'

'Father – why don't you say what you really mean?'

'I need time to think, Prakash. Or have we lost that right as well?'

'Prakash darling,' interrupts Rebecca squeezing his hand again. 'Don't make a scene. Your family is lovely.'

Prakash shakes his head. 'Will you come to the wedding?'

He stares at me, and then at Anita. Getting no response adds to his irritation.

'Treat everyone the same? He says. 'God created all men equal. It's all hypocrisy! Here's the news: I don't want any of you to attend my wedding.'

'Who said we'd come anyway?' Sanjay replies, 'I have nothing against Rebecca, she seems nice enough, but you must face some bare facts. Why should we lose our family prestige, because of your stupidity? Why must we accept western culture and lose our identity?

'You're so old fashioned, brother,' said Prakash. 'Times have changed and it's about time you came out of the time warp. We're in the 21st century, not the 16th!'

'Hear my answer, Prakash. Even if parents come to the wedding, my family will not. I cannot accept it. I don't want *my* identity washed away. I don't want *my* religion watered down. Your marriage will be a bad influence on *my* children.'

'Boys please, this isn't the time or the place,' I said. 'I'm sorry, Rebecca.'

Rebecca stares at her lap.

'I blame you, father,' said Sanjay rising. 'You've always spoilt him, and this has been the result.'

'It's not me who's spoilt, brother,' said Prakash rising as well. 'You're out of date, and I want you to apologise to Rebecca.'

Sanjay looks around the room, and then walks out without another word. Anita rushes out after him, calling his name.

The disaster I half feared has come true. What a mess. No one's on speaking terms. Prakash phoned later; he'll never forgive us if we don't attend the wedding. Rebecca is apparently inconsolable and he never wants to see his brother again.

The only person I've noticed with any sort of normality is Mother. Dare I say it, but there seems to be a spring in her old legs. I think I heard her singing the other night; having started the argument with her stupid beef roast, she feels quite pleased with herself. The idea of sending her to a Home, with spacious gardens suddenly looks very appealing. She feels vindicated about how things are turning out – she always said that if we lived here long enough, white people would marry into the family.

We will attend the marriage, even if Sanjay doesn't. Rebecca is a lovely young woman. One has to move with the times; otherwise one is left behind and ignored.

My father said I had become an English babu. Maybe he's right. I like my castle. Of course I've retained fond memories of India and visit as much as I can, normally in wintertime; the summers are still too hot. I've noticed a lot of people have no great fondness for their original motherland. And why should they? Hasn't England provided them with a good standard of living, with law and order? For all its faults, the country and its people have been welcoming and considerate. And I value gratitude very highly. Our migration has been successful on the whole. The losses are replaced with other values whether one likes it or not. This is what must happen when one crosses the seven seas to come and live in another land.

# Settled for Love

## by Hua Zi

―――

"I CAME TO this country to vex Larry – well, ini-initially."

Seeing the puzzled looks from my audience, I knew that my truthful one-liner wasn't going to satisfy their curiosity. But giving a detailed account at the book-promoting event would have seemed much too self-indulgent. In any case I was unsure whether I could speak to a group about Larry without losing my self-control. I was feeling overwhelmed by the publicity following my prize-winning poetry collection *Un-belonging*. Suddenly people were showing so much interest in me, wanting to know about my life: why I came to and settled in Britain, and so on. It was too much after two decades of peripheral existence as a first-generation immigrant. So to put a stop to questions being asked at future events, I decided to write my story down. After all, writing is what I now do for a living.

\* \* \*

Larry was among the early arrivals of 'foreign experts' teaching English in Tianjin. Our paths crossed when he came to QinYuan College in 1980, where I was a junior lecturer teaching Chinese poetry, following my recent graduation from the Teachers' Training College. I've often thought how accidentally people meet each other. Larry and I would never have met had China not re-instated the college entrance examination in 1977 after an eleven-year break. I was among the first group of lucky students admitted. For ordinary Chinese people, the re-opening of colleges and universities following the Cultural Revolution was a ray of light after an intense dark night. Without that re-opening I would probably have remained in a small village 90 miles west of Tianjin and Larry could certainly not have been a teacher in China.

We would have gone through life not knowing of each other's existence.

Simply knowing each other would not have ignited the relationship between Larry and myself, had I been of a different character and up-bringing. The fact is, once I've made up my mind to do something, I go for it. At that time, 'big-noses' – as we call western foreigners – were rare in China. Besides Larry, there were only two other westerners in our college, who taught Spanish and French; the three of them were accommodated in a compound at the southeast corner of the college campus and us young Chinese teachers at the far northwest corner. This arrangement was designed to restrict contact between foreign and Chinese teachers. Back then the authorities still viewed all foreigners with suspicion; social contact between them and Chinese citizens was strongly discouraged. Intimate relationships were extremely difficult and much disapproved of. However, all unmarried teachers lived inside the campus in those days. For us, not only were jobs assigned but also our meagre accommodation, which often had to be shared between same-sex teachers.

It must have been quite a culture shock and difficult for the foreign teachers to settle in, as facilities in China were pretty basic. They must have felt lonely – being so far away from their family and friends, from a richer and freer country, on top of the language and cultural differences. Yet the foreign teachers seemed friendly and eager to know us. Not all of us were brave enough to defy the authorities and respond to that friendliness. But I'm used to doing what I like, that's probably why Larry soon became my friend.

I was brought up by my widowed grandma in a small village. I never knew my parents – my mother died giving birth to me, there was not a single photo of her available. People in the countryside back then rarely had the means to have their pictures taken. My father was never mentioned, for reasons still a mystery to me. Sometimes I thought maybe he was a rapist and I was the tarnished result of an unspeakable shame. But such an image appalled me as I pictured my mother as pure and beautiful. Why else should Grandma often say that I was as beautiful as my mother? Other times I imagined my father as her forbidden lover whom my grandparents greatly despised. The fact that my mother lost her life because he made her pregnant would have sufficed to banish him. And Grandma must have had extra reason for hating him, because Grandpa died from grief only two years after my mother. "She was his sweet little girl," Grandma told me, "they were very close." Whatever the reason, I never managed to dig that knowledge out of Grandma. I asked some of the villagers about my parents, but all they knew was that Grandma and I settled there after the Yellow River flooded in July 1959. "Terrible disaster, that was, many places were totally wiped out, two million people lost their lives," they would say. "Thank heavens you were only a toddler, too young to remember it."

Grandma passed away a month after I graduated from college. Looking back, I'd the feeling that poor Grandma had held herself together purely for my sake, so as soon as I was on my feet, she was gone. Words from her last few days are still fresh in my mind:

"My dear, I'm proud to have brought you up well. You've got a good education most women can only dream of. That should secure you a good job. Now I can go to your grandpa and your mum in peace."

She didn't live to hear what my job was.

Grandma adored me and allowed me the freedom to do what I liked – so long as I didn't hurt myself or neglect my school work. I had a free, roving childhood without any parents' ever-watchful eyes. Not surprisingly, I turned out to be quite a tomboy and had a great time hanging around with the boys. We roamed the woods, hunted for nests, rambled around fields gathering anything edible, or simply trudged idly along the river banks skimming pebbles. What we liked most was to catch cicadas and locusts and roast them on a log fire. They were so delicious that I still miss them now. When I got home, my clothes were often a mess, but Grandma never reproached me. She would ruffle my short hair and ask whether I'd had a good time. On the whole I did whatever pleased me at the time and was quite used to having things my own way. Other village girls my age were never as free as I was and most of them were betrothed in their late teens and married off soon afterwards by their parents. If they had gone about as I did, their parents and future in-laws would have been alarmed; but thankfully nobody seemed to be bothered or nasty about me. Perhaps they felt sorry for me having no parents.

We were not well-off by any standard and lived as most villagers did then – a very basic material life. Yet Grandma never denied me things and always made do with whatever she could put her hands on to satisfy both my needs and my curiosity. She encouraged me to learn and discover things. I loved school, probably because of her instilling the urge in me to know. Grandma never failed to show how happy she was when I came top of my class in the end of term exam. Somehow she always managed to give me a boiled egg to celebrate my success. It was such a rare treat. I studied even harder after my first egg award, to please Grandma and to win another egg at the end of the next term.

Grandma was capable and hard-working, though she was rather thin and small in stature. She made all our clothes and shoes; no one in the village had money enough to buy ready-made ones in those days. I loved the shoes she made for me with a tiger face on the front – "it's to protect you against evil spirits," she said. Grandma was a wonderful cook, using mostly wild vegetables gathered from the fields. My favourite dish was the steamed dumplings stuffed with a wild vegetable called JiJi Cai. There were no heating facilities back then and during winter our northern province was extremely cold. Grandma would heat up a brick in the stove when cooking our evening meal and then wrap it in an old towel to keep me warm, the hot ash immediately being scooped into a metal container to warm herself. Whenever I think of these things I still miss my grandma terribly. In my memory, life with Grandma never left me feeling rejected. She was the only person who loved me wholeheartedly. At least I believed that until Larry came into my life.

Initially I never expected that we would get romantically entangled; though in my 20s, I had never had any romantic experience. Nor had most other university women of my age. After all, we had only just seen off the 60s and 70s – two austere, puritanical decades, when women who dared to defy convention and 'love' in what was considered the bourgeois way were paraded through the streets, each with their name on a placard, along with a broken shoe hanging around their necks, and were called the nasty name – 'broken shoes'! Many on-lookers jeered at them despite being ignorant of their 'wrong doings'. These women's reputation would be so shattered that no decent man would want to be seen associating with them. It was also, in those mad times, inconceivable for Chinese people to mix openly with foreigners, as any such association would have been punished with a spell in a labour camp in some remote location, from which some never came back.

So when Larry first held my hand, I withdrew instinctively and looked around to check whether somebody might have seen us. He was hurt at first but gradually came to understand my fear. As time went on, we grew much closer, more intimate. My every nerve was inflamed by our kisses. I had never known such powerful, all-consuming emotions. I eagerly awaited more, yet dreaded that we were doing something very bourgeois, very wrong. Sooner or later I would be punished and might even lose my job. Where could I go if that happened? Grandma had been my only refuge. If I messed things up now, there would be nobody for me to call upon. Every time after we had met, I would agonise and reason with myself that I must stop seeing him. But it was too late, Larry had ignited a mysterious desire in me, it broke loose and ran ahead. All I could do was to shut out rational thoughts, for their bleakness was awful. Thus the happiness of our love and the fear of what might happen to my career and future made it a very bitter-sweet experience.

We did our best to conceal our frequent meetings, so as not to provoke a visit from the authorities. Weather permitting, we would meet after dark, arriving on separate buses at a point on the bank of Hai River, about four miles away from our campus. Winter time was easier, our woolly hats and big coats helped to obscure our features.

Otherwise, I would go to Larry's place. We never dared to meet at mine, in case my roommates reported me. One blustery wet day, thinking not many people would be out and about, we ventured further away from the college to the Tianjin ZuJieQu. As we walked through the historic foreign settlements, Larry pointed out which one was in the French style, which one the British and so on. That was all new to me and it was a memorable day; I loved Larry's patience with me despite my ignorance. Yet no matter how careful we were, we were sometimes seen by people who knew me. And my increasing absence from the dormitory led to sarcastic hints from my roommates. I became aware of tittle-tattle and name-calling behind my back; and then I was given a serious talking to by my head of department who urged me to sever the 'inappropriate' relationship. But our love was too well cemented for me to yield to any pressure.

During this period, Larry managed to teach me some simple English words and phrases. I had learned a little bit of English at high school but Mr Jin, our English teacher, was not really qualified to teach the subject. His English was self-taught, Russian being his main foreign language. He was pressurised into teaching us English only because there were no more qualified teachers available. The fact was that poor Mr Jin never succeeded in teaching us how to pronounce English words properly. With his strong Sichuan accent, even if we did learn the words from him, no one would understand our English anyway.

So when Larry first befriended me, I soon gave up my attempt to utter one more English word. As for the few words I did remember from Mr Jin's day, I had to write them down in order to make sense to Larry. Nevertheless, we did have some fun giggling at the misunderstandings resulting from my brave efforts, writing such things as "I like you for your royalty" or "put chilly powder on the shopping list". In the early days we therefore tried to converse in Larry's somewhat better 'broken Chinese' rather than my unintelligible English. As time went on, we both felt keenly the language restrictions under which we tried to convey our thoughts and feelings; we firmly resolved to teach each other our mother tongues. But with our demanding work-loads, we could only devote limited time to that challenge and progress proved to be painfully slow, especially on my part.

What interested me most was when Larry talked about a life away from the only world I knew. He loved to talk about his hometown, Wilmslow, a village next to the River Bollin. He showed me coloured photographs of his parents tending their back garden, the house they lived in, the nearby woods, the river and the old cotton mill, the parish church across the road from his parents'. It was the church where he used to attend Sunday school and enjoyed Boy's Brigade activities – things I'd never heard of and couldn't quite grasp, despite straining my imagination. Growing up under Mao's reign, we were never exposed to such things. The government then viewed religion as emblematic of feudalism and foreign colonialism, and those who dared practise Christianity or any other religion were persecuted.

I loved the greenness and the tranquillity captured in those photographs – the variety of trees and bushes, sheep grazing in fields of long grass, the winding river. But what attracted me most was the people on a smooth lawn dressed all in white, playing a strange game Larry called cricket. So he used a ping-pong ball, chopsticks and a wooden cooking spoon to show me how the game was played. I also liked the red brick buildings; they looked so compact and pretty compared with the large, grey concrete ones that dominated Tianjin. All in all, Larry's Wilmslow reminded me of my grandma's village, even though houses there were earthen-walled with straw-thatched roofs. Since I had finished college and settled in Tianjin, the fields, trees and meandering river had become a luxury I no longer had access to unless I went to visit Grandma's village. But with a busy job and Grandma no longer alive, I had not been back there as often as during my student days. So when Larry talked enthusiastically about us getting married soon and how in a few years' time we would go to live in his hometown to be near his parents and the greenness I adored, I gladly fantasised – and of course feared – what it would be like to live among many golden-haired, blue-eyed 'big noses'. It was a terrifying picture yet exciting for me to romanticise over. Larry and I laughed about improving my English first before we could embark upon such an up-rooting for me; my perfect Mandarin, indispensable for us in Tianjin, would not be of much use in Wilmslow if I were to live a normal life there.

Those were such happy days; it came as a jolt to realise that Larry had been in China nearly a year and half. When the second long summer holiday came, Larry went back to Wilmslow to visit his parents; it was the longest summer holiday I had ever experienced. I had never thought one could miss another person with such agonising intensity. I counted each day with such impatience and listlessness.

On Larry's return I knew at once that he was not quite himself – he had changed in both mood and appearance. He was slimmer and less lively, almost too silent for me. Maybe he didn't really want to come back to China but felt obliged to. I became worried, really anxious that he was pining for his homeland after the recent dose of a more civilised life there. I supposed that homesickness was making him eat less of the Chinese food; he didn't have his usual appetite. When I felt homesick, I always missed the dishes Grandma used to cook for me. So I tried to look after Larry by cooking him a greater variety of dishes even though it cost most of my salary; and to cheer him up as best I could. I also tried to persuade him to see a Chinese doctor in case he was ill in some way. But Larry insisted that he was fine. It came as no surprise (though still a shock to bear) that Larry told me two weeks later he was going back to England for good. He had already resigned from his post and booked his flight. I was terrified that I'd have a life without him, without the only person I thought loved me, the most important person in my life since Grandma died. But Larry wouldn't change his mind about not staying any longer in China.

"Then how about we get married now and I'll go with you to Wilmslow?"

He assured me that he loved me; what we had was precious and as real as he and I standing in front of each other at that moment. But he couldn't marry me; he couldn't take me to Britain when I barely spoke the language and knew little of the culture.

"I can learn; I will learn anything as long as we can be together."

But my tears and pleading changed nothing. He seemed to have forgotten how eager he was barely three months earlier about the prospect of our being married. Larry left five days later and our marriage was out of the question.

I was devastated. At first I yearned for him with terrible intensity and seemed to see him everywhere. I had grieved a great deal at the loss of my grandma; but the grief caused by Larry's desertion seemed to be slicing my every waking minute, mutilating my heart. Within a month I lost twenty Jin in weight. Unable to sleep, I would go and sit in some quiet spot where he and I once sat, and weep over what we said and did together. When my roommates began to complain that my getting-up during the night disturbed their sleep, I would lie in bed quietly sobbing in agony so as not to offend them. I cried so much in the first few months, I thought I'd go blind. I was inconsolable; Grandma had been my only lifeline, and I could have talked to her about my longing for Larry. But there was no one living I dared trust. The pain and helplessness finally sucked me down and I was hospitalised for seven weeks with severe depression.

I received no news from Larry; the loneliness and emptiness were suffocating. But as time went by my feelings gradually hardened. I learned to control my heartache, though pangs of sadness still came over me – sometimes rekindled by the mere sight of something we had looked at together. But I never came to terms with Larry's abandonment of me, and my sadness began to give way to vehement resentment; later on to vengeful longing and hatred. It was awful that he had let me believe we'd soon get married and then so suddenly deserted me and left me with a 'reputation'. I was being laughed at and gossiped about by some colleagues and others who knew me. I would have changed my job to escape the hissing insults if that had been possible, but in those days whatever job one was assigned upon graduation was a job for life. My resentment and bitterness towards

Larry deepened as some people's ridicule of me grew more malicious. Finally I decided that enough was enough. I would go to England as soon as I could – I would eventually get myself settled in Larry's hometown, perhaps live next-door to him. Just to spite him and whoever he had chosen to marry instead of me.

We often hear of immigrants who have braved gruelling journeys here to escape war, torture, political persecution and other terrifying conditions in their home country. By comparison, my reason for coming might sound petty yet it was strong enough to motivate me not only to undertake the four-thousand mile journey to Britain but also to undergo five years' disciplined preparation for the trip. I did my best to learn English and to accumulate money – it was just as well that I didn't lose my job, probably only because of the severe shortage of qualified literature teachers at the time. It was an arduous preparation but I stuck it out and finally arrived at Manchester University in early September 1988 with a two-year student visa.

I could never have foreseen the shock I would encounter. I don't just mean the culture shock in general, and the ever-lurking homesickness well known to countless immigrants. I mean the personal shock of discovering what had become of the Larry I once loved and now hated in equal measure and had come all this way to vex.

I got off the train in Wilmslow at 10am on the second Saturday after I arrived in Britain. It didn't take me long to find the parish church and Larry's parents' house from the photos he had shown me. I paced up and down the pavement for a long time. I couldn't make up my mind whether I should summon up the courage to knock at that blue door, or simply hang around there for the day to see whether Larry might step out and bump into me. At one stage, I went inside the parish church and saw, for the first time ever, beautiful stained glass windows. The high arched ceiling, the screen far down the nave and many features I couldn't name all attracted me. I remember thinking I'd have enjoyed this had I been happy. But I soon sat quietly in one of the pews imagining that Larry was right there – doing his Sunday school and Boys' Brigade things. After a while, the footsteps of two visitors broke my reverie and I went to hang around his parents' house again. When dusk fell, I took the train back to Manchester.

Many thoughts raced through my head the following week. Should I travel around Britain and then return to China? I didn't really want to study two years for a Master's degree. Yet I felt it stupid to have come such a long way and fail even to get a glimpse of Larry. So I went back to Wilmslow the following Saturday. This time I was determined to go knocking on the door, no matter what embarrassment I might encounter or cause him. But as I approached the door, my courage again failed me. What if Larry's parents had moved? Even if they still lived in the same house, would he be there? If he had already married and moved away, would his parents give me his new address? Could I persuade them to do so? If Larry opened the door himself, could I honestly say to him "I came all this way to vex you"? Could I retain my self-control? If I broke down, would he invite me in and explain himself after more than five years' silence? I decided to go for a walk around the church-yard to calm myself and clear my head about what I was going to say when the door was opened. It was then that I spotted Larry.

Well, not Larry himself but his name on one of the family graves. The date of birth and the full name matched Larry's; the date of death was five months after his final return to Britain. I stood frozen, staring at the golden letters on black granite. My legs must have given way at some stage, for when I finally came to I was sitting dazed at the foot of the grave. The shock brought back the flood of emotions I had been through after Larry deserted me. I sat defenceless against the stabbing sadness, anger, grief, longing … I had no recollection of time, the day began to darken. I was torn between leaving Wilmslow forever and knocking on his parents' door. I now felt that his parents must still live there. But what could I, a total stranger, possibly say to them? They might never have heard of this oriental girl their son once loved. Had I any right to invade their grief over their only child? But could I live without finding out what had happened? Knowing that I never could, I finally knocked at the blue door.

I recognised Larry's father, though he looked a lot older than on Larry's photos.

"I was Larry's friend. I, I ..."

Larry's father understood quickly, saving me from further stammering, and asked me in. I was shown to the sitting room and introduced to his wife, sitting in a wheelchair. I thought of the elegant lady pottering about the garden on Larry's photos. I wanted to say something sympathetic but couldn't; I just burst into tears.

Larry was diagnosed that summer holiday as having final stage nodular melanoma, an aggressive form of cancer. He was put on treatment straight away. His mother had noticed the dark brown, dome-shaped scaly bumps on his legs and nagged him to see the GP to give her peace of mind. After exhaustive tests, a consultant confirmed that he had only a few months left. His devastated parents begged him not to return to China; they didn't want his treatment interrupted, even though they knew there was no hope of saving his life. But Larry insisted on returning, saying that he had to wind things up with the university and, above all, that he had to say good-bye to someone in person.

After Larry died, his parents found out about me from his diary and realised what we had meant to each other. How he agonised and couldn't bear the thought of bringing me over here and then leaving me to a language I barely spoke and a people I didn't know. So he thought the best he could do was to be cruel to be kind.

It took me several months to accept that Larry was dead. I then moved to Wilmslow so I could be near him and tend his grave. It gives me comfort just to walk along the village paths, thinking that he often walked there. The village scene also brings back fond memories of my life with Grandma and makes me really miss her. I have planted a maple tree for her on the north bank of the River Bollin and often sit beside it when I feel homesick. Life in Wilmslow is not always easy; but I have found inner peace despite my grief. Knowing why he 'deserted' me has given me much to think over. For a long time, I found it hard to deal with my remorse about the bitterness, even hatred I'd felt towards him. But I have never regretted my initial wilfulness, for had I not come all this way to vex him, I might have lived in anger for the rest of my life.

I managed to change my course of study to a diploma in professional nursing care, so I could help Larry's father look after Larry's mother. His parents have since become mine – the parents I never had. It was a sad fate that I lost him but I'm grateful to have found myself a family with his loving parents. Larry's mother and I have become great friends; and I can see that my help has made a big difference to his father. As my affection for his parents grew, I became ever more determined to apply for permanent stay in Britain, in order to be with them – and with Larry.

Looking back, I was probably granted the right to stay in Britain because of my nursing qualification – but I settled here for love.

*Published Poetry*
Hua Zi, *Marginalia*, Nede Press, Anona, 2004
Hua Zi, *Un-belonging*, Enivid Press, Cielo, 2007
Hua Zi, *Coming to Belong*, Enivid Press, Cielo, forthcoming

# The Escape

## by Qaisra Shahraz

N THE packed prayer hall of Darul Uloom mosque in Longsight, the Imam concluded the Eid prayers with a passionate plea for world peace and terrorist activities in Pakistan to stop. Seventy-three-years-old Samir, perched on a plastic chair because of his bad leg, kept his hands raised, quietly mouthing his own personal prayer.

"Please Allah Pak, bless her soul! And let me escape!"

Rows of seated men had arisen from their prayer mats and reached out to energetically hug others and offer the festive greeting, "*Eid Mubarak!*" Samir took his time. There was no one in particular he was seeking to greet or hug at this mosque. Most of the men around him were strangers and of the younger generation, several sporting beards – a marked shift between the two generations. His face remained clean shaven. Nowadays he prayed at the Cheadle mosque, joining the congregation of Arabs and other nationalities for the *Taraveeh* prayers during *Ramadhan*. Nostalgia tugging at him, on a whim, Samir had asked his son to drop him off in Longsight to offer his Eid prayers at his old community mosque.

Painfully rising to his feet Samir began the hugging ritual, smiling cordially. Unlike the others leaving the hall he loitered; in no hurry to get out. At the door he dutifully dropped a five pound note in the collection fund box.

Whilst looking for his shoes he bumped into his old friend, Manzoor – they greeted, smiled broadly and warmly hugged. Outside, in the chilly autumn day, his friend, who lived a street away from the mosque, invited him to his house for the Eid hospitality of vermicelles, *sewayian* and *chana chaat*.

The smile slid off Samir's face; he was reluctant to visit his friend's house – afraid of the old memories, shying away from the normality, the marital bliss of his friend's home. In particular he was loath to witness the little intimacies between husband and wife. The look. The laugh. The teasing banter.

Instead he waved goodbye to his friend and stood waiting for his son. "I'm being picked up," he informed a young man kindly offering him a lift home, before sauntering on his bad leg down the street.

"I have all the time in the world!" he wryly muttered to himself, savouring the walk down streets he had cycled and scooted along for over three decades. A lot had changed, the area now thriving with different migrant communities; the Pakistanis and the Bengalis living side by side with the Irish and the Somalis. Many Asian stores and shops had sprung up. The Bengali Sari and travel agent shops jostled happily alongside the Pakistani ones and the Chinese takeaway. Mosques catering to the needs of the Muslim community had sprung up, from the small Duncan Road mosque in a semi-detached corner house to the purpose-built Darul Uloom centre on Stamford Road. The Bengali mosque for the Bengali community on one corner of Buller Road was only a few feet away from the Pakistani and Arab Makki Masjid on the other corner. Not surprisingly on Fridays, for the *Juma* prayers, the street was gridlocked, with an occasional police car monitoring the situation.

He noted that the Roman Catholic church and its primary school on Montgomery Road had disappeared, joining the quaint little National Westminister Bank branch that had been in the middle of Beresford Road with a communal vegetable plot at the back. That had been pulled down twenty-odd years ago. St Agnes church was still there, however, at the junction of West Point and Hamilton Road and it still enjoyed healthy Sunday morning gatherings.

Samir stopped outside a shop on Beresford Road that had been called Joy Town twenty-one years earlier. It had been his children's favourite toyshop, especially on Eid day, when they ran to it with their *Eidhi* money, eager to buy cars, skipping ropes and doll's china crockery sets. In its place there now stood a grocery superstore with stalls of vegetables and fruits hogging the pavement area. On Fridays and Saturdays families, like Samir's, who had moved out of the area still returned to do their shopping, visiting their favourite halal meat and grocery stores; carting boxes of fresh mangoes, bags of basmati rice and chappati flour back to their cars. The hustle and bustle of these shops always bought out a smile in him.

His son, Maqbool, a well-to-do sports wear manager, dutifully returned to pick him up half an hour later. By that time Samir was shivering with the autumn chill in his *shalwar kameze* and *shervani* and gladly got into the warm car. He had wanted to go to Sanam Sweet Centre to buy a few boxes of Asian sweets to distribute to friends but he hesitated, suddenly overcome by trepidation.

"Do you want to go somewhere else, Father?" his son asked, as if reading his mind.

Samir shook his head; loath to inconvenience his son further, feeling guilty for already taking up enough of his time.

"No. Let's go home," he murmured, eyes closed.

He had a large five-bedroom detached house but with his wife and family gone all the joy of living had fled. He kept himself in the master bedroom, hating to enter the other rooms in the house, especially the one with his wife's clothes. Only when the grandchildren visited did he unlock some of the doors. He spent his time in his new favourite spot, the chair at the dining table next to the window and radiator. He sat there leafing through *The Times*, the *Daily Jang* and *The Nation*, watching the traffic go past on the busy road.

His son dropped him off at the door with the words, "Will collect you in an hour's time." Samir nodded and watched him drive away before letting himself into the house. Another hour to kill. He shrugged. It was better here on his own, with the TV and the news-paper keeping him company, than politely waiting around at someone else's house for dinner.

He felt hungry; but the dining table in front of him lay dismally bare. On Eid days it was normally stacked with bowls of delicious food: boiled eggs, *sewayian*, *chana chats* and a hot tray of *Shami kebabs*.

And these were just the breakfast starters, heralding a busy festive day of eating.

Last year his entire family had been there. If he closed his eyes he could see his children helping themselves to the food, with him happily beginning the *Eidhi* money-giving ritual. Five-pound notes for the little ones, ten for the older teenagers, and crispy twenty-pound notes for his daughters and daughters-in-law.

In the steamy warm kitchen with the noisy fan purring away at the window, the smell from a pot of pilau rice and trays of roast chicken and kebabs in the oven would set everyone's mouth watering. Dinner was a prompt affair; always at one o'clock, served by the women of his household, moving elegantly around the room; their rustling *ghrarars* and *lenghas* sweeping the floor and the long *dupattas* hanging at their sides. The boys would be in their *shalwar kameze* and *sherwanis*. By two, the whole family would be sitting around the table chatting, relaxed and happy, some still spooning away trifle and *gajar halwa*.

The thought of all that food set Samir's stomach groaning. He could not wait that long. In the kitchen he tipped some cornflakes into a bowl; it was not *chana chat* or *sewayian* but would keep him going.

He twice checked his pocket for the money, mentally counting the number of notes he should have. This was the bit of Eid day that he particularly enjoyed, glimpsing the excited faces of his grandchildren taking the *Eidhi* from his hand. In the old days a one-pound coin delighted his children. After dinner they excitedly ran off to Joy Town to buy gifts of their choice.

When Maqbool arrived, Samir was well into his second hard-boiled egg, smiling sheepishly at his son, who mentally chided himself for leaving his father to eat alone at home.

Samir's whole family was gathered in his eldest daughter's house and he was the last to arrive. In the living room his second daughter-in-law, Mehnaz, stood up out of respect to vacate her seat for him.

"Stay seated, my dear," he offered, perching himself instead on a chair near the door. The women were busy in the kitchen, sorting out the crockery and the sauces. All had happily adopted the British custom of bringing a dish since their mother had died. His eldest daughter was carrying a tray of roast meat through the hallway to the dining room. Catching her eye Samir smiled politely.

His youngest grandson Rahel jumped into his lap, startling him and bringing a smile to his face. Samir lifted him up to offer a tight hug. Then holding out a five-pound note he beckoned to his older grandson, a six-year-old, who was stood scowling a few feet away. The child shyly sidled to his grandfather's side, plucked the note from his hand and ran off.

"Would you like something to eat before dinner?" His daughter came to enquire, the blender with the mint sauce in her hand.

Samir shook his head.

Nodding she disappeared into the kitchen leaving Samir to smile, watch, listen and respond where appropriate. That is until the seat became too uncomfortable for his bad leg, forcing him to take the one vacated by his eldest grandson near the window. He bleakly stared out through the net curtains, watching passers-by, who probably had no idea that in this Muslim home they were celebrating *Eid ul Fitr*.

Eyes filling up Samir kept his face averted towards the window; there was nothing to celebrate on his first Eid without his beloved wife. Sorrow suffocated; desperation tearing at him. If he could only turn the clock back. How he longed to have this Eid dinner at his own home and with her hosting it, instead of sitting awkwardly here as an interloper.

An hour later he dutifully spooned food into his mouth, making no comments apart from the polite "everything is very nice" to the women of his family. He did not pick on the chillis or criticise the curry sauces as he had always done with his wife's cooking. His sons, of a different generation and attitude, were happily munching away at their roast meats, whilst he stealthily hid a raw bit of chicken leg under a napkin on his plate.

By the time the *gajar halwa* and tea were served Samir's mind was made up. He waited; heartbeat accelerating. When there was a lull in the lively conversation he ventured to inform his family, licking his dry lips carefully.

"I want to tell you something …"

They turned to stare. His daughter, Roxanna, hushed her little girl sitting on her lap with the words, "Abu ji is speaking, shush!"

"I want to go back home – to Pakistan," Samir announced, "to visit my family … stay there for a few months. It'll be good for me … it's the right time … with your mother gone … I need a change of scene and I have plenty of time now!" he explained, smiling. "It would be lovely to visit some places of my old life. Also good to spend some time with my sister and brother and their families."

Complete silence greeted his words.

"A few months! Are you sure about this, Father? We'll miss you!" His eldest daughter had found her tongue.

"You'll all be fine without me. Anyway, you can phone me every day …You've all got busy lives and families, so it won't be that bad to have me disappear for a few months. I'll hardly be missed … This trip will be good for me … I need to go …" He stopped himself from saying, "I need to escape", voice petering away, giving them a glimpse of the abyss inside him.

Discomforted and not knowing what was the right thing to say, they prudently ended the discussion. Their father had always made his own decisions – very rarely paying any attention to other people's opinions. Their mother had battled for years to influence him, and died having never quite succeeded.

"Where will you stay? Lahore?" his youngest daughter Rosie, boldly asked.

"Yes! In our family home of course, with my brother – where else?" he replied sharply, annoyed at his daughter's question and semi-hostile tone.

Rosie did not bother answering. Instead she covertly exchanged a pointed look with her sister, which their father neatly intercepted. Samir's face tightened. "You need to understand, Rosie, that just as this is your family – I have the same back home … They care about me and want me to spend time with them." His tone harsher than he intended.

The words 'back home' had just slipped out of him again. It was a curious use. For a few seconds he was lost in thought. Why did he say that? Was Manchester not his 'home'? After all, he had spent over forty years of his life in this city. The other place was just his birthplace, his country of origin and reminder of his youth. Surely these facts should make Manchester his home?

He shrugged these thoughts aside, willing his mood to lighten; he had a goal: to preoccupy his mind with tasks, and he loved tasks above all. The big task facing him now was what presents to take for his family and his two college friends in Lahore. He promised himself that this time the three friends would treat themselves to a walk through the tall elegant Victorian corridors of the Government College of Lahore where he had studied.

Three days later Samir had flown out from Manchester airport, taking his 'other family' in Lahore by surprise. They gushed with greetings, hurriedly assembling their shocked faces even though inside they were all amok. "What is he doing here, all of a sudden? How long is he going to stay? Which other relatives is he visiting and for how long?" These questions battered simultaneously in all their heads.

Samir's face fell, quickly averting his eyes, astutely picking up the tell-tale signs from their faces and body language. Two days later, after visiting the local Anarkali Bazaar, taking a leisurely walk down the famous Mall Road, and spending time with his sister's family in her villa in the Defence area, he headed for the village where his parents were buried. There he was amicably greeted by his host, a second cousin, who hosted all relatives visiting his parents' graves.

After some refreshments Samir headed for the cemetery on the outskirts of the village. Well maintained, tall tanglewood bushes grew around it, keeping the wolves out. Eyes blurred, Samir gazed down at his parents' graves. His father had adamantly made it clear that he did not want to be buried in the overcrowded city cemeteries. "I want fresh air, shade of a tree and plenty of space around – and make sure you leave space for your mother. Don't just throw us in any hole!"

As obedient sons they honoured their father's wish and duly visited the village of their father's ancestral home and bought a plot of land. Thereafter his sister and brother made annual journeys to the village, to offer a feast and *hatham* prayers for their parents' souls.

Samir perched himself on the low wall circling the plot with his parents' graves. The tranquillity around him had him thinking about his own burial place. Of course it would be Manchester's Southern Cemetery. He could not imagine his children traipsing back to Pakistan to visit his grave in a land that was foreign to them. He now understood why his father was insistent on keeping a place for his wife. Remembering his Sabiya, he bowed his head. The loneliness crushed. He ached to have her back. Two years ago they were both here, sitting at the same spot.

He watched a herd of milk buffaloes being shepherded back to the village. Feeling a tiny bite he looked down at a line of ants running down the brickwork. Laden with small scraps of leaves, the ants were zigzagging around his feet. He moved his foot away and glanced over his shoulders at the brick-making quarry and kiln, spotting a group of peasant men pushing trolleys stacked with bricks. Two women were carrying small baskets loaded with baked bricks on their heads. Feeling sorry for them and the hard work that the women had to do in order to feed their families, Samir was reminded of the second mission that had brought him to this village – his wife's charitable work. He had to visit the widow.

He turned to look back at the graves, taking his fill, etching the picture in his head. Was this going to be his final farewell? Standing over his mother's grave, soft sobs shook his large body. It was a strange world. To be buried continents away from one's own parents. Why was he crying? For his parents who had died decades ago or for his beloved Sabiya?

"Life is a cycle!" he mused. He was in his seventies but still demurred from being called 'old'. God only knew where the rest of his ancestors were buried – most probably in India, before the partition. People were born and slid through the cycle of life and then disappeared, with some leaving no trace.

"Samir stop thinking like this – it's morbid!"

He raised his hands to say a final fervent prayer over his parents' mounds.

His host family had gone to a lot of trouble in their offer of hospitality. The women had begun scurrying around the courtyard the moment he arrived. A hen had been snatched from the chicken coop in the far end of the courtyard and quickly dispatched to the cooking pot. The rice for the lamb biryani had been soaked. The pink custard powder was energetically whisked in a bowl. Not content with the home cooking for their special 'velati' guest from 'London', the host had enlisted the help of the village cook. A fabulous chef, it was widely said that people always licked their fingers after eating his tasty chicken shorba.

The women had happily obliged. Mina, the daughter-in-law, was seven months pregnant, expecting her first child, and hated squatting on the floor whilst cooking, on a pedestal stove. As well as that she had to maintain her modesty; it was quite challenging, keeping herself well draped in front of the male guest. Her pregnancy was causing her a lot of embarrassment. She was 'huge', everyone kept telling her.

With a last lingering glance at his parents' graves, Samir followed the path to the village central square with its old majestic looking Minar tree where his driver was waiting. His brother had kindly loaned both their driver and the car for his use whilst he used his motorcycle. Ahead of him he saw a young man pulling a suitcase and dragging something else.

Bemused Samir stared wide-eyed, temporarily transported to another time and place. He still kept his bedroll canvas bag in his garage in England, never having had the heart to throw it away. It was a memento, a part of his life. Too many memories were caught up with it. The frayed brown leather suitcase, stuffed with all his important documents, including his British nationality, was still kept under his bed.

There are special moments etched on people's minds; for Samir it was the one of him dragging a big bedroll and a large suitcase from Victoria coach station through the streets of London, deeply mortifying to this day. Why his arm and fingers did not fall off still amazed him. Tired, hungry and harassed, he and his friend stumbled thankfully into a Victorian house with a Bed and Breakfast sign; two Pakistani migrants from up north wanting to try their fortunes down south in London.

It was actually his friend's breezy confidence, smart use of English, cocky winsome smile and flirtatious winks that had successfully got them a room late at night, winning over the elegant old lady with her purple rinse. The purple hair colour of many older women in those early days fascinated him. Why did they like such a strange colour?

Samir shuddered, tasting the raw fear he had felt then as they desperately sought a place for the night. "What if we don't find a room, where will we go and what will we do?" He had silently agonised, panicking at the darkness falling around them . It was his friend's optimism and high spirits that had saved him from making a fool of himself. There was a moment he was ready to squat on the pavement and shed bitter tears, bewailing his stupidity in leaving a warm room and a cosy bed in Blackburn.

Sharing a double bed with his friend capped the humiliation of that day further. His friend had joked at their sleeping quarters and went to sleep soundly. Samir had sidled to the edge of the bed, shivering in the thin, coarse blanket making his face itch, afraid to pull it over himself and of waking his friend. In the end he had got up and pulled out his own five-inch thick Pakistani quilt from the bedroll.

His love affair with the English capital was both doomed and short-lived – it was not for him – too anonymous. He knew no one and felt shy and uncomfortable wherever he went – stumbling and stammering over the carefully chosen English words and phrases he had mastered to buy bus tickets, packets of Benson and Hedges or to order something to eat. Intimidated by the huge buildings and mad evening traffic, he smiled when he saw brown faces, mainly of Sikhs and Indians. He did not come across many Pakistanis.

After taking some souvenir photographs with an expensive camera he had brought from Pakistan, posing in his smart suit in front of one of the Trafalgar Square lions and outside the Buckingham Palace gates with the guards, Samir had happily fled. He wished his friend well with his love of London. Years later when he came across him he laughed aloud. His friend had become a true Londoner, down to the cockney accent.

For Samir, London was simply too much, making his life a misery and stripping away his self-esteem. Lacking his friend's confidence, easy-going manner and ability to make new friends, Samir missed the cosy comfort of a small town like Blackburn. After two weeks he had escaped, happily dragging his bedroll and his brown leather suitcase with him.

He went to another friend, who welcomed him with open arms, letting him join two other tenants in his two-bedroom terraced house. Apart from the kitchen all three rooms were used. Even the front room had a single bed hogging the area near the window and the open coal fire. That was the owner's room. The kitchen, with its big coal fire warming the room, was the hub of their communal life, where they took turns cooking meals, smoking and chatting, lounging on hard wooden chairs around a small kitchen wooden table. Three of them had young families in Pakistan.

Samir stayed put, intent on earning money to support his family back home by doing overtime and long shifts. *Keema lobia* became his favourite dish. He became a good cook, very proud of his culinary skills. His first chappati painstakingly rolled with a long empty sterilised milk bottle was a good try. His three fellow home mates praised him heartily, rewarding him with the teasing words, "Your cooking is better than our wives' back home!"

His landlord found him a job in the cotton textile mill, after he was pressured to turn down a job in a special nursing home in Darwen.

"You will be working with mentally ill people, are you mad? You'll become mad yourself!" His fellow tenants had cruelly scoffed, frightening him into scurrying into the reception room and leaving a hurried note to say no to the job before he had even started.

In the Darwen textile mill the huge dark machines intimidated him; but he quickly mastered the skill of working with and around them. It was dull and demeaning work. With his good education behind him he often heard himself dryly echoing, "If Abba sees me doing this, he'll have a fit!" His father had forked out a lot of money for the fees for a top college and expected him to do a 'clean' respectable office job, not working in some 'grotty' mill as his youngest son once termed it years later.

The pay packet, however, had kept him smiling. The thrill of counting the bank notes through the little top corner, and feeling the angles of the six- and three-penny bits through the brown paper, and the occasional half crowns – small sums but mighty big pleasures they provided then.

In those frugal days they felt duty bound to keep each other in check; the talk then was always about 'going back home'. They were not here to waste money on luxuries or on themselves. Exceptions were only made for gifts for their children. Samir had not only his wife and one daughter to support, but also his father to appease, who had never forgiven him for leaving home and doing menial jobs in mills in '*Velat*'.

The only thing that could win over his father would be the building of a new house, to illustrate his economic wellbeing and to support his younger brother's family. Three years later, having had enough of textile mills and with his family having joined him, he escaped to the big city of Manchester and started his own manufacturing business. It was a time when knitwear manufacturing was a booming industry in the northwest and Ardwick had become a manufacturing area. Many Pakistani migrants entered this trade. Samir too purchased an old factory for his knitwear business. It was also a time of social and communal uncertainty. Enoch Powell had done his bit, frightening the host community with his racist speech citing 'the rivers of blood' and leaving the migrants in fear of being thrown out of the country. When the Ugandan refugees started to arrive in the early 1970s after their expulsion by Idi Amin, his friends were very dismal about their own fate in the UK, fearing that they too would be thrown out. For some the mission or the next urgent goal was to build houses back home to return to if things really got bad in England.

Unlike his friends, Samir had faith in the British justice system and its fairness. He never for one moment believed that something similar could happen in Britain. Unlike some of his friends his savings went not into a khoti or a villa in Lahore, but in gradually working his way up to a better standard of living for his family, progressing from a terraced house to a detached house in a good area. He concentrated on his children, their education and careers. And the decades simply slipped away, melting away his youth and gradually severing the links with his homeland. His retirement was forced on him; he did not welcome it.

Samir smiled at the young man with the suitcase and turned into the village lane to pay a special call. In the widow's home there was panic as the youngest of the three girls whispered to the others that a man from *Velat* was standing outside their door. When their mother spotted the foreign visitor she nearly fainted, but recovered soon enough. Bursting into sobs she stared at the husband of their benefactor, muttering behind the fold of her long shawl, and gushing the welcome greeting: "*Bismillah! Bismillah!*"

She owed a lot to this man's wife.

Her three teenage daughters had rushed ahead into their *bethak*, to make the room presentable. The crocheted-edged table cloth was quickly straightened and dusted, the mirrored beaded cushions on the leather settee hurriedly plumped up and the pair of knitting needles and women's magazine snatched and shoved under the table.

Red faced and brimming with pleasure, the widow led their very 'special' guest into their humble living room, with the walls lined with their best china propped on wooden sills. It was a quaint sight for him, reminding him of the old days when his father would take him to tour some village for a "taste of the other life and warm hospitality of the rural people".

Samir did not know what to say, both touched and embarrassed by their humility and behaviour.

"Please don't bring any refreshments, Cola or Miranda bottles or such – I have a bad stomach," he glibly lied, saving them the bother and cost of purchasing the bottles from the local village shop. "I just wanted to see how you all are – and how your daughters are doing. I know my wife always visited you - as she did with the other homes she sponsored ..." He stopped, eyes filling up, his Sabiya in front of him.

The widow again burst into loud sobs. "We are so sorry about your wife's death, she was such a wonderful soul and so good to us! We miss her so much, and she phoned us every month – calling us to the butcher's house to chat with us ... always checking that we had enough money for my daughters' expenses and enough grain!"

"Yes – she was a good soul! And we all miss her!" Samir lowered his head to hide his tear-swollen eyes. The widow touched by his grief, stared in wonder, mouth open, showing her row of uneven top teeth and two missing lower molars. She quickly closed her mouth in embarrassment when he looked up.

Samir looked at the girls shyly staring at him, and could not stop the outburst. His sobbing caused the girls eyes to fill up. They were used to crying from an early age. Their mother had become a crying machine and often they ended up aping her. Today they found the sight of this older man from England, crying over his wife, very poignant. He was thinking, "My wife has made a difference to these wretched girls' lives!"

Sobering, he wiped his cheeks clean with a tissue proffered shyly by the eldest daughter. As if reading his mind, the widow reminded him. "Your wife got my oldest daughter married, she helped us with the dowry ... here is that daughter... she's visiting us at the moment." Then her gaze switched to her other daughters. "Who will now finance these girls' weddings?" Poverty had forced her into straight talking, to unabashedly appeal to the good nature of well-off people like him.

Samir had thought ahead. His pension, even if he did not touch the rest of his savings, would be enough to support this household – an ideal way of honouring his wife and her dying wish. Her last words to all her children and to him had been, "Do not forget all the families that I've been supporting in my life – earn their heartfelt prayers by helping them. Don't forget to keep my register of widows safe. Don't let anyone die of poverty or ill health! Display your humanity and offer generously your *zakat*."

His eyes on the four heads modestly draped with dupattas, Samir meditated on one possible way for these girls to get out of this poverty trap and offered. "Sister, please educate your daughters … Send them to any colleges that you like. I'll pay all their fees and other costs."

The girls' eyes widened and lit up in wonder. The *Velati* man would do that for them! Go to the town college. The girls' minds were swimming. Their poignant looks and smiling faces cut him to his soul. His own children, including his two daughters, had been educated to the high degree level and had access to great opportunities. Did these poor girls not have a right to the same? He was suddenly struck and dismayed by the inequality of life. How some had everything whilst others simply worried about the next meal.

The youngest girl moved away from the doorway, as Samir's village host, who had followed him to the widow's house, entered the room. Catching Samir's eyes the host signalled to him that dinner was waiting. Samir hastened to add before rising from the settee.

"Don't worry about anything, sister. I'll take care of your financial situation and make sure that you get your remittances on time, including for the wheat. You have our phone numbers, Please phone for any extra financial help needed. I'll take care of the furniture for your daughter's dowries just as my Sabiya did for your eldest daughter … I have to go now and may Allah Pak look after you all!" He felt in his jacket pocket and shyly placed a three-thousand-rupee note in the youngest girl's hand, lowering his gaze in embarrassment in the face of their gratitude.

He politely followed his host out of the small courtyard before turning to look back at the girls shyly peeping out of their door. "This is their humble world!" he mused, "and I live in a large house all by myself." The thought terrified him.

He politely smiled to the other villagers that he passed in the lane. There was no one he recognised and no welcoming look of sudden recognition. And why should there be? He chided himself. He was over seventy years old – and so far he had not seen a soul of that age group in the village.

That night he returned to Lahore to his brother's family. Fear of hospitality had made him flee the village, afraid that if he stayed the night his hosts would incur the cost of breakfast and afternoon dinner the following day. He was familiar with their generosity and excellent hospitality. Already they had spent a lot on his behalf. Until the entire dining table was covered with plates of cakes, pastries, boiled eggs and parathas they would not be happy.

In his brother's home there was no element of guilt – no waiting upon ceremony. They knew what he liked, and so for breakfast his brother would fetch some warm *kulchas* from the local bakery and the tea would be supplied by his sister-in-law.

Drinking a cool glass of *Lassi*, Samir instructed the driver to take him back to Lahore, the city of his birth, the old Mughal capital of India. He wanted to call on the way at the famous Data Gunj Darbar, a favourite shrine of his mother. In his childhood days she eagerly took him to pay homage to the saint buried in the tomb, visited by thousands every day from all over the world.

Outside in the Darbar courtyard the *daig* men were fast at work, serving food from their big pots to the needy and to those keen to take the *tabark*, food offerings, home for their family. When the man distributing bags of pilau rice touched him on his arm Samir was lost for words and nodded, taking the bag of rice with him inside the building. In the large hall amidst the crowd of male and female devotees, peering through the open windows at the tomb draped with a green and gold embroidered sheet, Samir offered special prayers for his wife's soul, tears gushing out of his eyes. Then a prayer for himself. He repeated the word "escape" again.

As he sheepishly entered his ancestral home the mouths fell open of his brother's family. They had not expected him back that night. In fact they thought he was touring another city and here he was, large as life. Both parties energetically avoided eye contact. His brother's family quickly recovered. They had been lounging around on sofas. It was eight o'clock and the popular drama was about to be telecast. The wife and daughter began panicking. Was their guest fed or did they have to scurry to the kitchen to rustle up a meal for him? Reading their minds perfectly Samir wryly held the bag of rice in front of him.

"I got my meal from the Darbar, I'm sure it's delicious. Don't worry about me, just carry on watching." With those words he left them to their drama, before excusing himself. "I'll go up to my room and have a shower."

"Yes, please do!" His sister-in-law quickly offered with a toothy grin and orangey *sak*-stained lips, sitting down to enjoy the drama with her daughter.

He came down after nine pm, having given them time to finish watching their serial. In that time, he had showered, eaten the rice from the bag with his fingers and started to gather his belongings. They were expecting him and hurried to greet him, his niece standing up.

"Are you sure you will not want a meal?" his brother asked, not happy at Samir not eating.

"The *darbar daig* rice was wonderful. Good to eat *tabark* sometimes, it reminds us gently what life is all about – our stomachs. Getting food into our bellies is what we work for, don't we?" His brother cynically nodded, a director of a firm and now retired. He still had two daughters whose marriage and dowries he had to arrange. It was not just the matter of food for him. He envied his brother for having all his children wed and settled. No worries, saving that of having lost a wife.

Aloud he instructed. "Bano, go and make tea for your uncle!"

A smile fixed on her face, the eldest daughter left for the kitchen, whilst everyone else watched the news.

"Tomorrow morning I will check flight times." Samir slipped in the information whilst sipping his tea. Heads turned, TV forgotten, surprise written on their faces.

"What brother! Already? You've only been here for just a week!" The sister-in-law rushed to speak.

"I think a week is enough – time to go home!" he replied, a gentle smile peeping across his features as he remembered his daughter Rosie.

Dumbfounded they stared back at him, but did not challenge or question him further as to why. "He must be missing his children," his brother thought. Once more all heads turned to the programme. As the eldest daughter got up to take the cups back to the kitchen, she smiled at her uncle asking if he wanted some more tea. He smiled back; it was the first full smile she had accorded him since he had arrived. Then she surprised him and her parents further with her kind offer.

"Uncle, please give me your laundry. I will see to it before you leave."

"You stupid girl! Your uncle is not going yet!" Her father chided, red faced. "He was only saying it. We are not going to let him go yet."

His wife quickly echoed the same. "No brother, you are not going yet."

"Don't worry, Bano! I'll get my clothes washed at home," Samir said, surprising himself. Twice he had used the term "home." Was not this his home, the place where he was born?

Chastened and the smile deleted, the eldest daughter took the tray of crockery back to the kitchen. In the lounge her uncle from England had already decided. He stayed up for some more polite talk and then went up to his air-conditioned room. Picking up the remaining items littering the dressing table he threw them into his suitcase. His love affair with his city of birth was over.

On the plane he found himself sitting next to a man called Ibrahim, of his age group and size; both overweight and uncomfortable with the economy seats and the narrow leg space in front of them. After exchanging polite chitchat they soon got into serious talking and were onto the question as to why they were visiting their country of birth and youth.

"The homeland?" Samir ruminated over the term and shared his musing aloud with his fellow passenger, who had similar home circumstances, including being a widower.

"The one that you have just visited, or the one that you are returning to? The place where you have spent most of your adult life? Which homeland are you trying to escape from?" Samir elaborated, making the man's sun-beaten forehead groove into three deep pleats.

"Escape?" Ibrahim was disconcerted by the term. Samir nonchalantly went onto explain. "I am escaping back to the UK – and to a new home."

"New home?"

"Want to join me?"

The man looked blankly at him, wondering whether this was a joke. Samir, chuckling, went on to explain.

He returned home not having met the two college friends or walked down the tall nineteenth-century corridors of the Government College of Lahore. Strangely it really did not matter to him.

Two weeks after his arrival Samir had moved to an elderly people's home, leaving his five-bedroomed detached house to his four children but keeping his savings and shares to see to the needs of the family he had promised to support. He made a new will, instructing his solicitor that when he died one of his children would carry on supporting the widow and her daughters. He got his eldest daughter to phone the widow, to reassure her that he had not forgotten his promise. Social and cultural parameters had to be maintained. He was a man and would keep his distance from the widow and not compromise her honour, her izzat. They needed his financial help which his wife used to provide; now he would take over her role.

When he spoke to his brother on arrival in Manchester, he was asked when he would return to his homeland. After a pause Samir asked, "Homeland? Which homeland? I'm home …"An awkward silence followed. Then he had added laughing, "You can visit me next time."

A week later the friend he had met on the plane arrived with his daughter, carrying his suitcase. Ibrahim took the room three doors away from Samir's, his gales of laughter echoing down the corridor. Pure joy raced through Samir, lifting his spirit as he rushed to show his friend around the home, enthusiastically explaining and reassuring, introducing him to the other house guests he had befriended, Penny and Derrick.

"It's the right decision my friend. You won't regret it. Wave goodbye to loneliness and heartache … We are the new English *babus*, living in old people's homes, the ones we used to ridicule once upon a time! Meals on wheels for us now – we have worked so hard – time to enjoy ourselves now, hey?"

# The Man Mayo Forgot

*by Nicola Daly*

———

"WHY DID you cover him over like that?" a fresh-faced copper asked.

My cheeks flushed with anger. If they had known Frank Malone they would have known that he would have wanted his death taken seriously. He would have wanted his face covered. That is what they did in the old country as Frank called it, until the wake at any rate. Granted he might not have wanted to be draped in a tartan table cloth with stains of HP sauce on but I just picked up the first thing I could find in his messy bed-sit.

I stood there a few minutes silent, feeling like an idiot I was that confused. My mind kept turning over the story Frank had told me about a boy kissing the dead soul of his father or something.

"Don't I know your face?" the copper said.

"Jesus, all I did was ring you lot, I came round for a game of cards and I found him like that."

"I'll need some details from you," he warned.

"Look I weren't here robbing him or anything, he was a mate," I said.

Then this older copper walked in and saw me and asked "What are you doing here, Finnigan? I thought I told you to stay out of my sight."

I gave him a filthy look; all I wanted to do was to finish collecting up all Frank's bottles, beer cans and newspapers, get the place tidied up, I didn't like the thought of people thinking badly of Frank, he'd been good to me, you see. I wasn't that shocked when I found him there like that, he'd been ill for years. He drank too much, you see, and the doctors reckoned his liver wouldn't take any more.

I was told to wait in the doorway while they went to talk to the neighbours. I knew they wouldn't know anything, to them he was just the man from Mayo who got drunk and bought everybody a round in the pub when his horse came in.

I'd been going around to visit Frank since my gran died and they put me in a kids' home. I met Frank a couple of years later while I was doing community service. They sent me around there to do his washing up. It was all part of this scheme to get young offenders back into the community. Anyway, surprisingly Frank and I got on straight away. He wasn't like most folk; he understood me. Listening to Frank's stories about growing up in Ireland and how hard he had it as an immigrant in the 1950s made me think about my life.

"When did you last see Frank?" they asked me.

I had to think about that because I hadn't been going around there all that often of late. I'd got myself a job working in this warehouse. Frank had an old mate there and he fixed it for me. He was like that Frank, do anything for anybody. I think he was like that because nobody had ever given him a break. He had it pretty tough when he came here.

The last time I saw Frank he'd been dancing down Market Street with a pocket radio blaring out of his pocket and a mannequin in his arms but I didn't tell them that; I didn't want them getting the wrong idea about him.

"It must have been a couple of weeks ago, I came around to his flat to cook him a meal," I said remembering what had happened later when I finally caught up with him.

I was forever taking him back to the peeling walls of that bed-sit of his and forcing food and black coffee down him and when he was sober enough he would tell this story about the love of his life – Maggie, she was called. The story never got boring no matter how many times you heard it. I suppose it wasn't just about Maggie it was about him and how being poor had forced him to leave the country he loved almost as much as Maggie and come here.

He always began with "Maggie was pretty as a picture." Then he'd ferret around in his pocket until he fished out a photograph of a neat-looking girl with pearly teeth.

"We met at a dance, a dance was something special in Mayo in those days, nothing like you have in England, we knew how to hold a dance, I'd be there on my fiddle and Maggie'd be looking up at me, her red hair shining."

Then depending on how much he'd drunk he'd fall asleep for a few minutes and I'd have to nudge him.

"Her father never liked me very much probably because I was forever in some trouble or other. I was accused – although nothing was ever proved – of taking money from the Lourdes fund and that reflected very badly on me for years," Frank said.

"So tired of having no money or future I set out for England. In 1952 I wanted to be a cowboy; I'd seen the films and I was determined to go to America and be a ranch-hand. The only thing that stopped me was Maggie. I reasoned that England was nearer. I figured I could visit her and I was convinced if I made something of myself her father would let me marry her."

"So what happened?" I'd ask, looking at the picture of Maggie he had placed in my hand.

"I came to England as planned. I could hardly wait to get here. You see, I thought Ireland was as dead on her feet as the horses I backed but I'd underestimated her. I got the shock of my life when I docked and walked the city streets half the night looking for a bed. The Irish weren't all that welcome, there were signs in the windows reading "No Irish, No blacks, No dogs."

"I was miserable, the work was long and hard but the pay was better and I managed to earn enough to send money home to my family who were badly in need. I also put some by for the life I had planned with my Maggie."

"Maggie really was pretty," I always said that just to make him feel better. The truth was it wasn't that easy to tell from the yellowing photograph.

"Maggie wasn't just pretty, she was clever and she was headstrong too; she got herself selected by the health commission to come to England and work as a nurse," he explained.

"So you got together then?" I always asked.

"Hold on, who's telling this story? I need a drink," Frank would say.

As I poured him another beer he'd sigh and start up his tale again.

"Now, what you have to understand is the immigrant experience was different for different people, Maggie was a trained nurse and people respected her, she lived in a nurses' home. I, on the other hand, was sometimes spat at and called Mick or Paddy and accused of taking the job of an English labourer. This room was my lodgings and I shared it with three other people."

At this point in the tale Frank always tended to ramble a bit about the rough treatment he got on the various building sites and the only thing that kept him going was the occasional stolen hour with Maggie.

"I couldn't bring her here because if you think it's tip now, you should have seen it with three young fellows living in it and in those days a decent girl like Maggie would never have agreed to that sort of thing. We couldn't so much as drink a cup of coffee together in her lodgings because no men were allowed," Frank explained.

Frank laughed at this part of the tale and would start waffling about how he broke into Maggie's lodging with a piece of mistletoe and the matron came after him with a rolling pin.

"Now in all the time I've been here in England, I've never once gone home for Christmas. You see, whilst I miss those Mayo Christmases with twelve of us elbowing each other for a tiny piece of goose and Ma telling the same jokes and the priest nearly knocking the door down whilst we all hid in the cellar, the shame of never amounting to anything wouldn't allow me to go home," Frank said.

"Nonsense, you've loads to be proud of," I said.

Then gradually Frank would get back to the story.

"Just after I'd proposed to Maggie, she set her heart on going home for Christmas. She thought I should go back and speak to her father but I told her I wanted to get myself a job with better pay before I bothered her father but she thought I was making excuses and being head-strong and a little bit home-sick she went home without me."

"No, she never really understood why I felt so ashamed of never becoming the big success. Anyway, by the time she returned from Mayo I could tell that I was losing her piece by piece; she was gradually growing more and more distant. I thought it was her family to blame at first but then I realised she had met somebody else in Mayo."

Tears would appear in Frank's eyes as he said, "My own cousin John. She claimed she missed the horses and the autumns in Mayo but I knew she was lying, Now about this time I began drinking heavily. Things weren't going too well for me. I was caught stealing the petty cash from an office I was working in as a tea-boy and then there was the incident with the Baby Jesus and I think this was the last straw for my Maggie," he said.

"Why, what did you do?" I prompted

"It was my last Christmas with Maggie and she was depressed. I thought it was because she was missing her family and English Christmases are nothing like a good Irish one. She couldn't go home because she was working and kept complaining about the dreary nurses' home and how it looked naked without any proper decorations. This was what gave me the idea to go to Midnight Mass after the pubs closed and see what little trinkets I could pick up."

"What did you pick up?" I asked.

"A beautiful nativity figure of the Baby Jesus. Of course, Maggie was as mad as hell about it, she wouldn't see me for weeks, then she sent me this letter," he would say, standing up and pulling the cushion up on his arm-chair to reveal a grubby envelope.

He never tired of reading the letter to me even though it must have hurt. Sometimes you could see the tears in his eyes when he read the line

"'I never meant to hurt you but it is for the best, I fear my family were right about you, I am often disappointed by your behaviour.'"

Even the last time I saw him he was talking about Ireland. I don't think he really left, not in his heart anyway; he read Irish newspapers, drank in Irish pubs with Irish people.

"Ireland is like a huge theme park and there is no place there for the likes of me. They've forgotten us old codgers; we were the ones who got Ireland back on her feet by sending money home. Besides, I lost all contact with my family after Maggie married my cousin John."

"Didn't you ever meet any English girls?" I asked him

"They came and went but there was nobody like my Maggie," he would say.

Then I'd turn off the electric fire, put a rug over his knees because he'd usually drifted off to sleep and then I'd let myself out. Like I told the coppers before, he sorted me out with the job, he was family. I'd go back the next day and he'd be sat there lonely and drunk. When he was really feeling sorry for himself he liked to tell this story he called 'The Man Mayo Forgot'. It was about this guy called Patrick who couldn't go back to Ireland because he had nothing to offer his family and he was too proud to live on charity. I knew it was about him even though he changed the names and the locations. I never let on that I knew, though, because somehow I sensed he wouldn't have liked me feeling sorry for him. Now though, I wished maybe I had.

# Long Journey To Love

## by Valerie Bartley

———

ONE SIZZLING hot afternoon, Mamma, pregnant as usual, was gasping for lemonade and dispatched me to the shop to buy sugar and a slab of ice. I noticed that she seemed to have a rare fancy for lemons, but I kept my trap shut in case I lost a tooth to her left hook. As I set off, she spat on the ground.

"Straight there and back before that dry up!"

I didn't stop to ask what she meant. I ran all the way.

I was served by a man I had never seen before. He asked me my name.

"Valerie," I told him.

With a dazzling smile he said, "A lovely name for a lovely girl. Where do you live?"

"Old Walk Lane." I pointed in that direction.

"When are you coming to the shop again, Valerie?"

"Don't know." I was irritated by his interrogation.

"My name is Eric, I'm going away to England soon. I would like a nice girl like you for a pen friend … you know, someone to think about."

I thought it was a curious way for a total stranger to introduce himself, and to say such an upfront, articulate thing. However, I was only sixteen, as green as the bananas on the trees and forever being told not to let boys touch me. He was just a fellow with adorable wandering eyes, and a trap that flew open easily. Mrs Bedward sat under the tree, scrubbing away at her washtub. I thought he must be her relation, but I was too shy to ask and sprinted down the lane, remembering the spittle drying on the ground. Gasping for breath, I reached home just in time to see the froth succumb to the shimmering heat. My close encounter became a passing moment. A few days later I was busy scrubbing the floor, when Mamma called.

"Valerie! Go and get me some sugar so I can make lemonade; my throat is burning." She gave me the money. "If they have any ice, get a pound."

I flew off like a kite in the wind, and again was gasping for breath when I reached the shop. Eric was stocking the shelves.

"Who is chasing you?"

"No one," I panted. "One pound of sugar, please."

He looked me over. Shabbily dressed in an old frock, with dirty hands and knees from scrubbing, I felt embarrassed, knowing I looked as if I had just blown in from a refugee camp. Again he mentioned writing to me from England, our *mother country*, as we referred to it then. I suddenly realised Mamma hadn't mentioned the spit, but I knew the rules; my life could be made hell with her spit watch.

Eric's words rang in my ears. I'd never met anyone so ambitious. Excited and extremely flattered, I was out of breath when I got home. Mamma was shelling gungo peas surrounded by the fowl.

"Who you a ran from?"

I dropped the paper bag. All this time she'd been sending me out with the warning not to let the sun dry up her slobber before I got back, and never once noticed that when I came back I could hardly breathe. All those times!

I decided to tell her about the man at the shop, who said I was a lovely girl. But before I could tell her about his plan to go to England, she looked up at me with eyes bulging out of their sockets.

"What man? When me sen' you out, you don't stand chatting to no boy, you me?"

"Yes, Mamma."

"Lord me God!" she said, springing up and scattering peas all over the floor, giving the chickens a feast. "If you ever let them touch you, I'm a going to turn you out a the yard with your bundle, and you can go to the woodland and live under the stone cave with the ratbats!"

She changed her clothes and stormed off up the lane like a goose on the run, while I stood there in shock. I never moved a muscle until she returned; she must have erupted like a volcano while she was there, as she came back much calmer.

"Well," she said, plonking her hands on her wide hips, "I told him you was far too young for him, and he should not talk to you and eye you up again. I tell you again; when me sen' you out an' you see boys, men or dogs that want fe stan' an' chat, you run home. You hear?"

"Yes, Mamma."

"An' you don't care what them say, you just run, because all them want is to get them wicked ways with you. Then when them breed you, them turn round and say them never touch you with a long spoon. Prevent is better than cure." She pointed her fingers into my face and I shivered with fear.

I didn't understand; I was quite shaken by her reaction, but Eric hadn't done me any harm. I only told her because I was excited at meeting someone who planned to cross the Atlantic, never believing I could meet someone so ambitious weighing flour in a shop.

I didn't see him again. Mamma sent my sisters to the shop, shielding me from the wolves and the long-tongue men. I tried to forget him and his talk about England. One glorious afternoon, Mamma sent my sister to walk four miles to the post office. When she returned I was shocked to find there was a letter for me. I never had a letter from anyone before, never mind a red and blue one. I was mystified by the name on the envelope; I couldn't recall anyone named Bartley, but before I could look at it properly Mamma shouted,

"Don't open it, put it between the wattle until me finish plaiting Evelyn's hair."

I didn't want her knocking me about for a red and blue envelope, so I did what I was told. As I chopped the wood, I wracked my brains; it might be from the man I met at the shop. I was scared, remembering how Mamma had exploded. I watched her through a hole in the kitchen wall, plaiting the last few strands of Evelyn's hair. Then she ripped into the letter with razor fingers, and her eyes popped out as she read it. When I saw her coming towards the kitchen I held my breath.

"It looks like Eric's heart still a burn for you. Look how far away he is and him still a boiling up for you."

My head was spinning. I wanted to read my letter, but didn't dare ask. I never thought he would keep his word.

Mamma held on to the letter. "Me a keep it till your father come home."

She stuffed the letter into the depths of her bosom, where it warmed and mellowed until Poppa arrived home. The sun was a vast orange, sinking fast in the distance and the chickens were going to roost. Mamma sat on the verandah, her face like thunder, watching as Poppa yanked the food-laden hampers off the donkey's back.

His voice was weary. "Evenin', Saida."

Mamma shuffled on the old wooden chair like she was sitting on thorns.

"What happen to you now? Why you swell up like that?" Poppa asked.

"Lord, sir, I don't know where to start from to tell you." She fidgeted again. "Valerie got a letter from Mrs Bedward's brother."

"Who?"

"The man from the shop that was eyeing her up."

"Which man?" he barked, scratching his head lividly as if a horde of lice had suddenly descended.

"The man that said he was going to England, where you always wanted to go." Mamma was transfixed as if in a dream.

"Oh!" Poppa said, swinging around. "So what you trying to do, open up old wounds? I never remember a thing about it."

Mamma refreshed his memory.

"So where is the letter? Read it to me!"

He watched as Mamma delved into her cleavage. She suddenly said to me,

"Go and light the lamps."

I rushed to light the lamps and darted back.

"No way will I let her go thousand of miles away to a stranger." Mamma's voice was raised to the sky and I knew what that meant.

Poppa cleared his throat. "I remember when they came here looking for people to emigrate to England after the war, and I had a burning desire to go but you said you wouldn't because you had no intention of flying in an aeroplane."

Poppa seemed annoyed, but Mamma just shuffled her bum in the chair. "And what happen if she go and he treat her badly? We no got no money to send back for her if things no work out."

Poppa's comments gave me a boost, and a rebellious feeling, too. I really wanted to explore the world, make a life for myself, and be free from this bondage and when I was finally allowed to read my own letter, tears of anger welled up. She had confiscated *my* letter. However, I knew I had to tread carefully as my parents held the knife handle and I held the blade, and if I grabbed it too fast I would surely get sliced.

Somehow, I found the courage to tell them I intended to write back to him. I needed to win them over to my side so I tried to keep calm. Many weeks passed before I was given the money to buy the stamp. I walked to the post office in the blistering heat, but I felt I was walking on air.

When Eric's reply came, my heart started to race.

*"My dear Valerie,*

*England is very cold even though it is spring. I felt like a block of ice, and was shocked to see huge fire balls in the houses when I arrived..."*

He was looking for a job, but without luck so far. He didn't paint a picture of how I imagined England would be. I knew the streets weren't paved with gold, but the Royal family lived there so I thought it would sound more exciting.

When I replied, I told him all the latest news and that I would love to join him one day. Eric told me how much he loved me every time he wrote. I found it flattering, but I didn't know what being in love felt like, or what love was. I hardly knew him. He found a job working in a Rochdale cotton mill for six pounds a week, but still found it hard to save the money for my plane ticket.

My normally law-abiding father and his brother joined in a group growing ganja and earned £20 each. He gave me fifteen pounds and I was very touched, promising myself that I would always remember the risks he took to help me out.

For two years we kept writing and then Eric told me get the ball rolling and apply for a passport. I made myself a lovely striped dress for the occasion. It was the first time I was ever photographed, but the pictures were fine. I sent one to Eric and he told me he slept with it under his pillow. I wondered what it would be like when we finally got together. Every time I read his letters I seemed to find new meanings in the words.

Then one day I woke up and I was eighteen years old. It was just another working day with no party or presents. I was old enough to go away, but not old enough to marry without my parents' signatures. It was hard but I kept going and hoped for victory.

Finally, Eric's letter came. He had finished paying for my fare, and the date of my departure would be 13th December 1961. I was so excited that I began to jump up and down, and then out of the blue Poppa and Mamma started to clap their hands. I almost died with shock, especially when Mamma jumped up and started to dance. I began to cry, as I never dreamed that I would see my mother showing such delight for me. I knew then that I was on my way, and although she didn't say a word at that moment, I could tell without any doubt that she was happy for me. She hired Uncle Eddie's truck to take me to the airport, and as the days drew nearer my heart was constantly beating like a drum.

One thing worried me a lot. No one ever discussed sex with me. It was taboo. The thought of it frightened me and I wanted some advance information. I gleaned a certain amount from other young people, but nothing specific, as we were all in the same boat. I wanted to talk to my mother about sex, but it was a dirty word and no one talked about it. It was as if they didn't do it. I plucked up courage and asked her if she had anything to tell me before I went.

"Oh me Lord," she said, rolling up her eyes like she just got the last rites. "I don't know what to tell you right now."

I tried not to show how desperate I was for her advice. I gave her the wistful look, but it didn't work. Her big brown eyes gazed at me in shock.

"When you get there, Eric will teach you," was all she told me.

"When you reach over there, if he no treat you right and proper, write and tell me," she suddenly exclaimed. "We no have the money, but we would have to borrow from your Uncle Eddie and send back for you."

On Sunday, 13th December 1961, I woke to the sound of the usual funfair outside. The cocks were having a glorious time. I could hear them crowing and Hanna braying. I stored the memories in my mind to take with me. Mamma was up early, busying herself in the kitchen as Poppa tied hibiscus flowers to the rope around Hanna's head. I was thrilled that he took the trouble to dress her up for my last ride to the main road.

I slipped into my new brown dress with six buttons down the front that found curves I did not know I had. Mamma prayed to God to guide and protect me, and wished me a safe journey to the unknown. I walked out into yard, taking in the surroundings for the last time before I set off on the first leg of my journey to England and Eric. Up on Hanna's back I felt like the queen on her throne. Poppa plonked my brand new case with my few belongings on his head, while Mamma stood waving until we were out of sight. Tears misted my vision as Hanna carried me along the road that we had walked together so many times. When we reached the main road, we were picked up by the truck that would take me to the airport. I stroked Hannah's neck and looked around once more.

As the truck driver skipped around the potholes, I stood up and looked at the tropical beauty I was leaving behind. What would life be like in England? I knew that it would be cold, but not a lot else. My head was spinning one moment, and the next my heart was pumping my left melon so hard I thought it would explode.My emotions were mixed; sadness that I was leaving all my family behind, and joy that I was about to embark on the adventure of my life. A journey to the unknown, six thousand miles away. Thoughts of Mamma rushed through my mind, as she had decided to stay behind and pray for me, saying that she couldn't bear to watch me fly off like a bird in the sky.

When I came back from my thoughts, the truck had turned into the road that led to the airport. Poppa's eyes moistened as he took me and my suitcase to the check-in desk. He held out his free hand to me, as if he was guiding me to heaven, but he knew that he was sending me off to a world unknown. I was given my one-way ticket and British passport back by the serious-looking clerk. My hands were shaking and for a moment I just wanted to turn and run. My father kissed me for the first time that I could ever remember, and wiped his eyes with a handkerchief already soggy.

After a long delay, we were told the flight was cancelled because of bad weather in England. I wondered if my family was still upstairs waiting to see my aircraft roar down the runway. We were put up in a hotel in Kingston. I was sharing the room with a lady in her thirties called Beryl. We had only the clothes we wore, because our luggage had gone on board. We had a cooling drink and freshened up, smelling bewitchingly of the lavender soap in the bathroom. I had never clapped eyes on such things before and it was a great treat to me, so I washed my panties with it and hoped that the beautiful smell would last throughout my journey.

We slept in our birthday suits, and when Kingston burst into life the following morning, a bus took us to the airport. It was the beginning of a new adventure of my life. I was nervous and really frightened when the plane started galloping faster and faster down the runway and finally took off into the sky. The turquoise sea shimmered below my window seat. I watched until there was nothing to see but blue sky, and the drifting clouds, whiter than Mamma's treasured bed sheets. I thought of my family back home, and the journey ahead, and prayed in my little brave heart that we would reach safely to the other side of the world.

We landed in New York some hours later and were allowed to leave the plane. It was very cold and, with no overcoat, I had a taste of what was to come.

I never thought England was so far away, and that it would take so long to get there. It was certainly the longest journey of my life, and it was the same for all of us who were making our first jaunt into the unknown. There were people praying openly, and I said a few prayers myself, and was comforted knowing that Mamma would be bruising her knees at her bedside.

When the plane hit turbulence I was like a scared cat, gripping the sides of my seat. I was also bursting to go to the toilet, but was terrified that when I opened the door I would fall out into the sky. Beryl was equally frightened. She was joining her partner whom she hadn't seen for over two years. But at least she knew what to expect when she and her fellow were reunited. I wished I could pluck up the courage to ask her about things.

When I sensed the plane dropping out of the sky my heart seemed to jump out of my chest and I felt sick. Then suddenly the pilot said the magical words, "Ladies and gentlemen, we are about to descend to Gatwick Airport. Please fasten your seat belts. We hope that you have enjoyed your flight and we look forward to seeing you again."

My feelings were mixed as the plane descended from the sky. I prayed that it wouldn't crash like a coconut falling from a tree. Would I recognise Eric, I wondered? Would he remember me? I had grown since the first time he clapped his warm brown eyes on me at his sister's shop. I hoped he was armed with the small passport photograph that I sent him, otherwise he might miss his Jamaican princess when she walked through Customs and into his arms.

When the plane finally touched down on British soil I was very relieved. There were some people shouting, "Thank you, Jesus," and others clapping their hands, thanking the Lord for bringing us safely to the promised land. We had been travelling since Sunday, and it was late Tuesday night when we arrived at Gatwick Airport. Confused and disorientated I was unsteady on my feet, drunk with tiredness.

I came down the steps from the plane like a sheep wandering to new pastures. The wind, biting my face, was the only welcome in the damp, pitch-black night as I lugged my suitcase along like a pregnant mare pulling a cart up a steep hill. Walking the endless corridors in a trance, I was gripped by fear of the unknown and unnerved by the glaring eyes that relentlessly bored into mine.

Other people in the queues looked just like me … all turned out in our Sunday best, but we must have looked such a sight amongst those dressed in normal working clothes, and they stared at us as if we had dropped out of space.

We were waiting to be questioned by the immigration officers. I came through that easily enough and then, interrogation over, they dropped the bombshell. A Mr Bartley had left a message for me. Because of the delay, he'd had to return home to his work commitment. I was to take the train from Euston to Piccadilly Station in Manchester.

I nearly died when I was given the message; panic and fear took over my whole body like a raging fire. The delay had ruined his well-planned arrangements. Some people were lucky and hugging their families who had waited for hours to meet them, but I was a frightened eighteen-year-old; alone in a strange country, bewildered, exhausted and scared witless. The stiff, bitter wind almost blew me off my feet, and I felt it punch at my bones as I tried, in the dark, to read the signs telling me where to go.

When I arrived at Euston the last train to Manchester had already sneaked off without me. I missed my connection, and it was fortunate that I had struck up a friendship with Beryl. She was going to the Midlands, wherever that was; it didn't mean anything to either of us. We sat up all night at Euston Station and again I was shaking with fear; it would be the first time my feet ever touched a train, never mind my backside kissing one of the seats.

I was not used to seeing so many white people and there seemed to be lots of people living rough around the station area. There was one man who was very scruffy and dirty. I later discovered that he was a tramp. I had not imagined that there would be such people in England. At home we would call someone like him Nasty Nagger. He struck up a conversation with us.

"Like your 'ats," he said, grinning at us.

We didn't answer.

"Ain't you cold?"

We still didn't respond but we must have appeared to be freezing, draped in our thin cardigans, and I was trembling with fear and the cold wind that was kissing face.

Beryl gave the vagrant a mango in the hope that he would bugger off, but he stood there tearing into it like a lion with his first kill of the day. He continued talking as he ravished the fruit.

"You foreigners?"

We nodded our heads in acknowledgement but never uttered a word.

"Come with me, I could get you both a coat."

We were horrified and exchanged glances, still without speaking.

"I don't know 'ow you could leave bright sunshine to come and sit down 'ere in the cold all night. I'm used to it, but it ain't easy."

I prayed that he would go away and leave us alone.

"Must be bloody mad!" he declared, nodding his head and scanning us with his eyes. Then he picked up several cigarette butts and stowed them away in his pockets.

"Got a light?"

"No," we replied in unison.

"No bad 'abits?" he asked. "Good gels?"

There were a few trains sweeping in and out of the station and his voice was drowned by the clanking and hooting as they passed. He vanished as the station came to life with the early commuters arriving, and very soon it was bustling with people. By now I was blue with cold, and so stiff I could hardly move.

Finally our train swept into the station; we boarded it and breathed a sigh of relief, glad to be on the next leg of our journey. We sat close together, barely daring to speak as we chugged along. Beryl was going to Birmingham and we were sad to say goodbye. We didn't even exchange addresses, as we had no pens. We told each other the address we were going to and I thought I would remember, but the cold icy wind blew it out of my brain.

It was another long journey. I sat looking through the window at what I thought were a lot of factories, with my pillar-box hat just the same as it was when I first laid it on my head when I had left home.

As the steam train juggled along, I looked at the countryside; the leafless trees; their branches waving in the wind, and the darkening sky without even the promise of a ray of sunshine. I felt desperate and drew on my last reserve as I sank lower into my window seat. I had always been hungry for adventure, but I was so exhausted from travelling that it began to get to me. I was badly in need of a bath, too, after three days dressed to kill in the same clothes. Oh Lord … how much further?

Finally, I arrived at Piccadilly Station, and walked out into the cold, driving rain. I didn't know where I was going and kept walking through the bullets of shiny rain until I got to a taxi stand and asked for 27 Scarsdale Road in Victoria Park as I had been told to do.

When the taxi dropped me, I looked around, making sure that I was knocking at the right door. I knocked and knocked but no one answered, so then I started to shout, "Is anybody in?" but there was no reply. I was so very cold, and beginning to panic. I looked down at my suitcase and it stared back at me. Close to breaking down, I knocked again but still there was not a soul in sight. Just as I began to despair, a lady came out from across the road and looked me up and down.

"Have you just come up?"

"Yes," desperation echoed in my voice. "But there's no one in, I have been knocking for a while now."

She started to bang on the door like she was trying to waken the dead, but still there was no reply.

"You better come to my house, and I will come and knock again later."

She picked up my case and led me across to her open door. I was so grateful that I couldn't stop saying thank you.

"It's okay," she said. "No problem."

I stumbled through the door behind her in a state of shock. Had I been set up? What if I couldn't find Eric?

In the living room, a roaring fire startled me; I had never seen that before in a house, but I sure didn't complain. It was wonderful, a delightful welcome to a lost, frozen soul.

"Sit down, let me make you a cup of tea," she said, switching the wooden box off. I'm not ashamed to say that I didn't know what that was; I'd never seen a television before. I noticed a baby propped up in a dry bathtub in the corner of the room surrounded with cushions to keep him steady. A toddler sat close to him looking at me with big eyes.

The woman soon returned with a piping hot cup of tea, a hunk of bread, and a piece of fried fish. I bit into the bread and fish in a flash and as I hugged the cup, I could feel the heat seeping into my hands.

"Well, I didn't even get the chance to ask you, what is your name?"

"Valerie."

"My name is Melda." She smiled warmly. "How was home when you left?"

"Fine." I told her I left home on Sunday, but with all the delays it had taken three days to get here.

"Really? You must be very tired." She sat in an armchair next to me. "So you have come to the mother country, Great Britain!"

"Yes ma'am," I said, and took another huge bite of the bread. I asked how old the baby was and she told me he was four months old and his name was Vinroy.

I thanked her for the food, feeling so much better.

"No problem, it's a pleasure," she said

Melda got up. "Let's go back and see if his morning has come yet."

I didn't understand.

"It's when you work nights … when you wake up in the evening, that's your morning," she explained.

I thought it was strange, but I got the message at last and she went ahead to see if Eric's morning had arrived. After a few minutes she came back smiling, and told me that this guy came to the door in his pyjamas. She asked him if he was expecting somebody from home and he said yes.

"You should have seen his face. He had the widest smile I have ever seen on someone in pyjamas," she said, with a burst of laughter.

"I asked him to tell me your name, and he said 'Valerie.' Well, I said, she is in my house."

I jumped to my feet, trying to control the relief that I felt, and wondering what we would say when we came together at last. Thanking Melda for her kindness, I walked out into the cold, dark night with my case, leaving the welcoming fire behind me.

The moment that we had been waiting for had come at last, and as I walked up to the door I could see a small figure standing in the hall. There were a few more heads popping up behind him, struggling for a glimpse. Eric flung his arms around me, and asked me if I was okay. I told him yes, but in reality I was a nervous wreck.

He said, "I'm sorry we never heard the door knocking, John and me finished our night shift this morning and was fast asleep." He turned to the other two guys standing in the hall. "This is my girlfriend that I been telling you all about."

"She's very nice," one said.

"Pleased to meet you," the tall man said, shaking my hand. "My name is Earl."

"I'm Valerie." I felt shy and awkward.

"The day I came to Gatwick to meet you, I worked the night before and had no sleep. I came all that way only to be told you were still in Jamaica." Eric nodded as he spoke. "Anyway, I must have drifted into a deep sleep, and that's why I never hear you knocking."

"I'm sorry to cause you all that trouble, but it was because of the bad weather."

"That's quite okay," he beamed, and gave me a warm, gentle hug. "You were worth waiting for, I'm a lucky man."

I saw the two other men's faces peeping from their room doors, as Eric held my hand gently and led me upstairs to his room. I told him that I was cold.

"Never mind. You with me now, we are together at last," he reassured me.

The room was huge, with a high ceiling and tired wallpaper. He drew up a chair for me and I slowly lowered my backside on it as I surveyed the room, relieved that we were together at last. He held me close to him and kissed me for the first time. I had never been kissed before and it felt like heaven as my body started to melt. My heart fluttered frantically like a butterfly caught in a jam jar. That first experience was spectacular, really mind-blowing, and the memory of it will never leave me. It was like my first taste of chocolate, my first trip on the aeroplane, and my first taste of alcohol all rolled into one. I wanted more but he slowly released me and said he would make some tea.

His bedroom was cold and I felt the chill as we walked inside. I couldn't understand why steam spouted from my mouth like smoke every time I spoke. I watched him light the fire while I galloped into a mug of piping hot tea and warmed up my half-frozen body. Fire in a bedroom ... I thought, my God, what had I done, leaving the Caribbean behind for this? The small wardrobe seemed lost in the big room while the huge dressing table, waiting for the adornment of my trinkets, and the two Victorian chairs gazed at me. The multicoloured lino that covered the floor had finished its days long ago. My hands were dancing, as I tried to hold the cup.

"You must be hungry? I'm going to make something for us to eat," he said, changing from his pyjamas into a pair of khaki pants. I sat motionless, watching the fire spitting, as the spiral of smoke curled up the chimney. He returned with two plates piled with sliced potatoes, eggs and beans. I dived into mine with delight.

When I finished eating, he held my hands, stroking them, and suddenly I felt a warm glow seeping through my whole body like a slow-burning flame.

"You are beautiful, even more than the first time I saw you," he beamed.

I smiled shyly and didn't really know what to do or say to him, but I was beginning to enjoy his comments and his touch immensely.

"That was lovely, thank you," I said, trying to change the subject and pushing away the enamel plate that I was quite used to at home, but never thought I would see in England, of all places.

Suddenly there was a knock at the door, which made me jump. It was Earl. He just wanted to gawp at me.

"How was your journey?"

I told him, but I just wanted to be left alone for a while to compose myself and soak up my new surroundings. Eric announced that he had to get ready for work.

"Work?" Earl's face registered shock and disbelief. "You will have to take the night off, man. How could you leave her and go to work? You must be mad. No work is better than what you have here tonight."

Eric smiled, but didn't say a word, and my face turned blood red. When Eric decided to take the night off I cannot say that I was delighted; I just didn't know what was best, as I had no say in the matter.

Earl stood up and stretched his long, lean body. "See you tomorrow, Uncle."

I was dying for a wash, and felt that a bath would do me the world of good after going without for three days, but I still felt chilly and there was no central heating in those days. I took my nightdress in with me to hide my embarrassment. When I came out of the bath, my teeth were chattering again. I lingered for a moment to gather myself together, but there was no mirror to throw the last moment of innocence back in my face. I wondered if he would be kind and let me sleep till morning came. I began to panic, my heart was thumping and my nerve was about to burst when suddenly there was a knock on the door.

"Yes, who is it?"

"It's me, Eric. Are you okay?"

"Yes," I answered, gathering up my clothes. I took a deep breath before taking the few steps to his bedroom.

He was perched on the edge of the bed when I walked in. I didn't want our eyes to meet as I felt so embarrassed to be alone with him. I laid my clothes on the chair slowly one at a time.

Eric held out his hands and I went into his arms; he kissed me gently.

"You have grown into a lovely young lady, haven't you?"

Our bodies met and I smiled nervously at his comment, and slid quickly beneath the sheets. My mind was blank as he tried to make love to me, but it was difficult, and terribly uncomfortable. I was very scared and my hair stood up on my head as he persistently tried to burst my bubble. I thought it would never end, but when it did I wondered what all the fuss was about ... the earth never seemed to move under the bed.

We must have fallen asleep wrapped in each other's arms, and the next thing I knew was the first chink of dawn peeping through the window, and my frisky stallion was lying beside me. I was lost under his armpit and wrapped up like a snake in heaven. I awoke feeling like a woman for the first time.

When we finally rose, he pulled the thin dark curtains and let in, not the sunshine that I was used to, but the dark grey morning. He lit the fire to keep me warm.

Getting to know each other took some time. It was important for us to talk and we wanted to share all our thoughts. The day went in a flash, and before I knew it, night came again but as far as I could figure out, it had looked like night all day. John was sound asleep in our bed, while we talked the day away. He was moving to his own room as soon as he could find one, but for the time being we had to share the bedroom. We had little privacy, but we were used to hardships and difficulties, and helped each other out as we were all in the same boat.

That night they went off to their night shift, leaving me alone in our cold, silent room. There was no radio or television, so I wrapped myself in the blankets and watched the embers of the dying fire until I fell asleep.

I woke several times, feeling strange; I wasn't used to having a bed to myself. The house was serene and it was the same outside; no crickets or frogs playing their music all night long. It was like the middle of a graveyard. My mind was working overtime and I felt afraid.

"Is this it?" I asked myself. The illusion of England I had in my mind didn't add up to what I had seen so far. I pulled the blankets over my head and sobbed until I heard a knock, and the key turned in the door. Eric was home and I was glad to see his face again. It was too early for me to get up and sit in the cold room, so I laid there with my warm body waiting for him and my heart suddenly beat faster. Eric climbed into bed and snuggled up beside me, with a wide grin on his face, as if I was a ball of fire waiting for him to thaw out with.

A few days later John moved into a room downstairs, and we were left alone to explore our new-found world of love, which was heavenly bliss. It wasn't long before we were making plans for our wedding. We didn't have much money, but decided that we would do the best we could.

On Saturday, 31st March 1962, we got married in Moss Side, Manchester, in the church at the corner of Denmark Road. I arrived ten minutes late, in my £200 Chantilly-lace dress, carrying a bouquet of roses and peonies. I walked up the aisle to the strains of the bridal march, thinking about my parents and the girl I used to be. I wished that my family could see me, but they were six thousand miles away, basking in sunshine while I shivered in the cold of the spring day.

When we came out flecks of snow were falling like confetti and a light blanket of snow covered the ground as a determined wind tried to swipe my veil away. We had just three wedding presents, as we didn't know many people, but we had a wonderful day. Eric held me close and told me how much he loved me, and hoped we would share many happy years together.

Man and wife, we danced the night away.

# How I Broke
# Mama's Commandments

*by Sue Stern*

———

AMA HAD given me her version of the Ten Commandments. It was neatly folded away in my trunk but she'd repeated the words so often before I left, I knew some of them by heart: Be careful of strange men. Do not give your trust too easily. Be restrained in what you say. Do not let yourself be carried away. That kind of thing.

In the Port of St Petersburg, waiting for our ship to leave, I stood close by the ship's rail, its metal tubing cool beneath my fingers, the sun warm on my face. It was May; soon would be the time of the white nights. Mama said this would be the best month for my journey. However long or hard it might be, the dark and cold would not oppress me.

People were crowding around me; I smelled sweat, garlic, bad breath. A woman who'd been feeding her child, had wound him in her shawl and was standing so close to me, I could smell baby milk and rose water. Perhaps the mother had sprinkled it on the baby to sweeten it. I wanted to reach out and touch the baby's head but instead, I smiled at the woman and she returned my smile

'How old?' I asked.

'Six months,' she said proudly.

We stood closely packed together as the ship moved, seeing the sea ripple along the bows, the people with horses and carts on the quay becoming smaller and smaller.

A touch of melancholy overcame me: there was no-one on the quay to wish me a safe voyage, to embrace me in loving arms. My family was in Archangelsk, five hundred kilometres away.

'Goodbye again, Mama,' I whispered. 'You know I'll send for you when we have a place. We'll buy the tickets and you'll come to the Golden Land.'

I wanted this message to fly through the air, over the forests and the mountains, straight into her heart, so she'd sense I was thinking about her, the very moment I left Russia.

'Talking to yourself?'

I turned. A young man had edged his way through the bodies and was standing next to me. He smiled, raised his eyebrows.

'Or praying maybe?'

Fair hair, brown eyes, a good jacket – and he was older than me. I knew at once that I liked him.

'Not praying,' I said quickly.

'Yet all around, they are.'

He swept out his arm. He was right – the men with long beards, the *chasidim*, were nodding, bending, muttering, their wives silent, shawls drawn closely over their heads. Even the less orthodox, who wore ordinary Russian dress – hats, shirts, long coats – were moving their lips too. The children stood silently for once, gazing towards the land, towards Russia.

I shook my head.

'So you're an atheist?'

I laughed.

'A New Woman,' I replied.

'Then a woman after my own heart.'

I glanced down to see if he was wearing a ring, but his hands were hidden in the pockets of his very elegant, brown jacket. Besides, it meant nothing. Usually only married women wore a ring; they were the ones who were bound, I thought to myself. Looking up, I saw he was smiling a wide smile; he had a dimple in one cheek which added to his quite handsome appearance. Careful, I told myself. This is only the beginning of the journey.

I turned to look out at St Petersburg, its churches with their golden onion tops, the white imperial buildings. My heart beat faster.

Supposing this was the final separation? Supposing I'd never see my family again? Now I knew why the others were gravely still or praying with fervour. How eager I'd been to reach the port after my days on the train. Even the overnight stop with Papa's friends in Petersburg had seemed like an irritation. The dark water slipped and swayed by the side of the ship, and I was afraid.

The man's voice came from far away.

'England or America?'

'Both,' I said. 'I'm meeting my brother, Sasha, in London. Then we travel together to New York.'

'Quite some journey,' he observed, leaning over the rail.

There was a sigh, almost the sound of a moan, as the people retreated from the ship's side now we were truly at sea. Children began to run around, a mother slapped a child and it cried; I needed to read Mama's words again, to be close to her.

'I'll go down to my place in the hold,' I said. 'I'm a little tired.'

'Of course.' Bending his head slightly, he held out his hand, 'Dov Feldman.'

'Sophia Kretchevsky,' I said, taking it.

'Very nice to talk to you, Miss Kretchevsky.'

As I descended, I thought about my mother, always patient with everyone, always hopeful, and about Papa who'd become morose over the years in Archangelsk. He hadn't been like that in Petersburg, Mama had told me. Now he was always ready to remind me what a feather pillow I had for a brain. Full of outlandish ideas, too much reading, and one day, he said, my learning would ruin me. The most ridiculous idea, according to Papa, was something I wanted for myself. It was to become a doctor. In Russia at that time, boys could, and did, go to university. Of course there was a quota, only so many Jewish boys were allowed each year, but as for girls, they could be school teachers or nurses, nothing more. When I reached America, I would be anything I wanted.

Full of these thoughts, I reached the lowest level, where it was so dark I could barely see to walk. Now I heard such screams, such dreadful moaning, my breath caught in my throat. A woman was in terrible distress.

Moving as fast as my skirts would allow, I reached the hold that ran the full length of the ship, and stopped at the doorway. On one side, at the farthest end of this dark, long place, were huddled all the men, their faces turned away. In front of me was a group of women, who'd made a kind of circle around a bunk so that the person was hidden, but it was from here that the turmoil came.

At once I wanted to run over, help this person, stop the terrible screaming. But I also wanted to fly back to the upper deck, to the open air, to escape. As I hovered, hesitating, a sturdy-looking woman walked steadily down the corridor towards me. Her blonde hair was hidden by a scarf looped under her ears and tied at the neck; I knew she was very orthodox.

'Take this to them,' she said. 'It's hot. Be careful not to spill it. I'm going for more.'

It was a bucket of steaming water and I had to carry it with both hands, anxious not to slop any over the sides. The women made way for me. It wasn't far, just across the deck. Nearing her, I was shocked to the core. A blanket covered most of her body but an older woman, kneeling on the planks beside her, uncovered the lower part and there I saw her nakedness, and the head of a child, crowning. I gasped, let down the bucket, which I'd almost dropped and pressed my hand to my heart, forcing myself to breathe deeply.

Another woman, her right arm tight beneath the woman's shoulders, her left gripping the woman's arm, was shouting, 'Push. Now. We can see the head.'

'I can't,' groaned the woman. 'I have no strength. It's finished. Pray for me.'

Her voice disappeared into a terrible groaning, which became a scream. I shuddered. But the other women kept urging her on, talking to her, entreating her, doing what my mother called 'Talking her in.' Which meant, in Yiddish, giving her the confidence to believe she could do it.

'Dip the rags into the water,' commanded the first woman, who'd returned. She had light, almost white eyes and wisps of fair hair emerged from under the scarf.

I did as she told me.

'Hand them to me.'

So I worked with the two midwives, if that's what they were, sometimes averting my face, yet desperate to see what would happen. I wondered how this pregnant woman had even managed to embark on the ship, so severe were the Russian Emigration Officers with their examinations and restrictions. The woman gave a grunt and a scream. The others prayed and cried and encouraged. And the child covered in blood and goo slipped onto the sheet. The pale-eyed woman lifted it up and gave it a smack. It began to cry. Someone took it from her and began to wipe it with wet rags.

All the women called, 'Mazeltov.'

'Quiet. She hasn't finished yet.'

She pressed her hand on the woman's stomach and the afterbirth, a pulsing mass of blood and veins and skin, emerged. She bent, and to my astonishment, bit the cord in two with her own mouth, then knotted it close to the baby's stomach.

'Now you can shout,' she said dryly. 'I was afraid she wouldn't do it,' she added, as though to herself.

'Why didn't you get a doctor?' I dared to ask.

'What, a ship's doctor, even if there were one?' She shook her head fiercely. 'Butchers, all of them. They'd have killed her, or the little one. Or both.'

'A boy,' the other women cried. 'You have a boy.'

Someone dipped more rags into the second bucket and washed the baby briefly.

'The water's getting cold. Enough. Let him have a warm beginning.' Another woman went over to the father, huddled with all the men, and he ran to his wife, shouting, 'A boy. A boy, thank God.'

The rest of the men slowly returned to their places and I sat down on my bunk.

The woman with pale eyes came over to me.

'Thank you,' she said. 'For a young girl, you did well.' 'Not so young,' I said. 'I think you may have been married at my age.' 'How old are you?'

'Nineteen.'

'Still young, but yes, already I had two children. So how did you manage to stay without fainting away? You saw your mother give birth?'

I shook my head vigorously.

'I do have brothers, one older and one younger, but I must have been at school when he was born.'

She nodded slowly.

'Still, you did well.'

Without a second thought, I told her about wanting to become a doctor. She stepped back as though I'd said something strange, even immoral.

'What about marriage? Your parents haven't arranged your wedding?'

I thought I'd better be careful what I told her. My parents were educated, modern people, and I assumed she was unlettered, even ignorant. But I'd misjudged her, she wasn't so easily shocked. When we introduced ourselves – she was called Ettie Gutenberg – and she discovered where I was going and that I was travelling alone, all she said was, 'If you need anything, any help, come to me. My bunk is there.'

'Near mine,' I said gratefully. She went back to her family and I lay down on my bunk. The woman who'd given birth seemed to be quite restored. I saw she lay feeding the baby, with the rest of her family gathered around her.

Thoughts spun round my mind. What Mrs Gutenberg would have called the Evil Inclination was sitting on my shoulder. We all have one, it's believed, and a Good Inclination, sitting on the other shoulder. There's always a choice. Well, my Evil Inclination was talking to me, asking me why women must suffer, why they must be punished when they bring a child into the world. Didn't Adam and Eve both eat the apple? So why did men go free? This was the kind of thing I was thinking and it was reinforced by the books I'd been reading, the literature Sasha had given me before he left. I wanted to leave Russia, not just because of the pogroms and the hatred of the Jewish people, but because of the injustice and poverty I saw and my yearning to change it. I wanted to heal the world, but in a different way.

After a while, when I'd eaten some of the bread and cold meat that Papa's friends had given me, I made a little tea. There was a samovar at the end of the deck, which we could use. I'd brought lemons; I cut a couple of slices and floated them in the cup I had with me for that very purpose. I took a cube of white sugar and drank my tea with the sugar between my teeth, and the sweetness and bitterness, combined, cheered me, making me feel strong again.

I'd completely forgotten about Mama's Ten Commandments, so taken was I with what I'd experienced, so full of thought and questionings about the rights and wrongs of it all. Now I took the sheet of paper from my trunk, pressed it close to my nose, imagining I could smell the lavender she always used, and read the commandments slowly. I felt better.

The following day I met Dov Feldman again. It was the evening, this time. Clouds moved across the sky blocking the stars, the moon appeared and disappeared. We were crossing the Baltic Sea, making for Riga, where more passengers would climb on board with their *perrones*, their feather bedspreads, and their trunks, and their children. I was glad of the wind, lifting the stench of the hold and the strange smell of the logs on the cargo deck. What was to become my place, by the railing near the end of the deck, was where he came to me.

'So, Miss Kretchevsky, are you enjoying the voyage?'

He was wearing a different coat, dark blue, with burnished buttons, and smoking a small cigar.

'Sophia,' I said. 'Please call me Sophia. And the voyage? I am learning a lot, I think.'

I told him about the woman giving birth, without going into detail, of course. And how kind the *chasidic* woman was, even though she probably disapproved of my travelling alone. Turning back to look at the sea, I shivered. Those hundreds of gallons of black water. What if something happened?

'Deep thoughts?'

'I can't swim,' I said simply. 'Although I know it's in the Torah. Teach a man a trade and teach a man to swim, and even some women are good swimmers, but not me ...'

He laughed.

'There's nothing to fear. A solid ship and fair weather.' He paused. 'Kretchevsky. That's a name from the Ukraine. Have you come all that way?'

'No, from Archangelsk.'

He raised his eyebrows.

'A woman full of surprises. Do you live in one of those wooden houses by the sea?'

I nodded.

'But from Petersburg originally,' I continued. 'We were forced to leave when I was five.'

'What a cursed thing.'

I was surprised by his anger.

'We must act. We can't let them treat us like slaves. Workers of the world unite!' He flung out his arm.

Just what Sasha used to say. This man, despite his air of wealth, his clothes – and where did he sleep, not down in the hold with us – this man was a revolutionary.

'Are you from St Petersburg?'

'Of course. All the best people come from there.'

There was such warmth in his manner, something roguish, engaging in his smile, I laughed and blushed at the same time.

'Then why are you leaving?' I asked to cover my embarrassment.

'It's a long story, Sophia my dear. But we have plenty of time.'

I was surprised when he called me *my dear*, but I soon learned it meant nothing – it was simply his manner. He told me how he'd been one of the leaders in the failed revolution only the year before. How he'd escaped imprisonment, or worse, by the skin of his teeth,

'Or by the thinness of the cloth in the coat I was wearing. When a soldier grabbed me, it tore away at the shoulder, and I managed to escape down a side street. A comrade hid me in her bed – imagine it – until the military gave up the search. When they swarmed into her apartment, she told them I was her sick, old mother and couldn't be disturbed. She was a pretty thing. I think they rather fancied her.'

He gave a great laugh. I blushed again. I hadn't heard such talk before, at least not about men and women. How naïve I was.

'Sasha has given me books to read. I've read *What Is To Be Done*?'

He gave a great shout.

'Chernychevsky! Excellent. And have you read Peter Kropotkin, the early socialists, Leo Tolstoy?'

When I looked taken aback, he said he'd lend me some books for the journey. Then we could discuss them!

So began my initiation into socialism. More and more, I looked forward to our talks, could not wait until we stood together by the ship's rail. Truly, I was a little in love with him. One day, after we'd left Riga and were travelling through the North Sea towards England, he caught my hands in his. I thought he was going to kiss me, and I made myself ready, my heart a bluebird, fluttering in my chest. But I was wrong.

'Don't go to America,' he beseeched. 'Stay with me in London. Come to the Anarchist Meeting House in Windmill Street, just off the Tottenham Court Road. It's called *Anonymie*, the club for radicals. You'll meet Rudolph Rocker, the great leader, not a Jew, but he learned Yiddish and has revived the newspaper, *Germinal*, after Zola's great work – '

'I've read some Zola – '

'Good girl. People all over the world are reading this journal right now. Live with me in London and we'll go to the meetings together. That's the centre for the new thought, that's where all the passion is!'

I hesitated. I didn't know what to say, torn as I was between my fascination with Dov and my need to go with my brother to America.

My conversations with him hadn't passed unnoticed. Another time, as I lay on my bunk, dreaming, Mrs Gutenberg passed by. She stopped.

'Take care, Sophia,' she said. 'Don't be caught by those dangerous words, his fine manner. By his charm. Think what your mama would say.'

She nodded several times, standing squarely next to me, her arms folded.

I recalled Mama's Ten Commandments, especially: *Do not let yourself be carried away.* She knew so well how words intoxicated me, how impressionable I was, despite my determination to be an independent woman.

I sat up.

'Maybe you are right to say this, Mrs Gutenberg. But we are only talking. There is nothing between us.'

'Even orthodox girls would lose their heart to men with clever words, if we didn't protect them. You are on your own. It is my duty to speak to you.'

I breathed deeply, wishing she would go away, leave me to my dreams, stop interfering with my life. She said nothing more, and I took one of Dov's books, and lay curled in such a way that nobody could see what I was reading.

When I used to sit daydreaming in our house in Archangelsk, Mama would ask me my dreams.

'America,' I'd tell her. Not for its streets paved with gold, I didn't believe such foolishness, but for the freedom we would have. We could say what we liked, when we liked. Not to be ever fearful of someone reporting us to the authorities.

'Remember, Sophia,' she'd say. 'Every country has its rulers and its rules. You have to observe them. Jewish people have always said that the law of the land is the law.'

I'd argue with her, telling her this made us subservient, that we needed to be strong. We never agreed. When I mentioned this to Dov, he told me how Rudolph Rocker and his lover, Millie Witkin, had reached America and being unmarried, were not allowed to disembark from their ship. Refusing to marry, Rudolph Rocker claimed that love must be free, or else it would be prostitution. They were forced to return to England. This rather troubled me. Not of course that I wanted to copy Millie Witkin, but somehow it diminished my regard for America.

'That wouldn't happen in England,' Dov said. 'Such a marvellous country. How broadminded and tolerant it is.'

People must have sensed something of this, because once we'd sailed into the English Channel, there was a change in their manner. Everyone talked cheerfully, we were almost carefree. By now the sea was grey, rarely blue. I was surprised the weather was so cool, that often there was rain, and cold winds swept the ship, even though it was nearly summer. Some of the passengers, like Mrs Gutenberg, were heading for London, where they had relatives, or what they called *landsleit*, people who came from the same village or area as they did. She'd given up trying to persuade me not to talk to Dov. Just frowned at me, waving a finger, when she passed me in the hold.

Others, like me, were going on to America, the Golden Land, as they called it in Yiddish. Not all the passengers were Jewish. There were Russians and Poles, Prussians and even Scandinavians. Everyone escaping poverty and hoping for a better life in England, or North and South America. Even, some said, in South Africa.

England, at last. Such excitement as we sailed slowly down the great River Thames, passing tall and tiny buildings, wharves and docks, boats and liners, just as along the Neva, in Petersburg. But how different. Never had I seen so many narrow streets of houses, all with smoke spiralling from blackened chimneys, even though it was springtime. We were aiming for Millwall Docks. Sasha would be waiting for me there. He knew the place because that's where he'd arrived in London some weeks before. I had his address carefully folded, safe inside an inner pocket of my bag.

There was a sudden silence as the engines stopped and the ship docked. Now all the passengers were crowding the deck, some smiling, others praying, this time with gratitude for having passed a safe journey. Mrs Gutenburg stood further along the deck with her family. Even though Dov and I stood together in our usual place, she waved to me, smiling, almost girlish, before turning back to look out over London. It was almost a blessing.

'Sophia,' Dov said suddenly. 'I'm sorry I couldn't persuade you to join the comrades in England. Fight the glorious battle. But in case you ever need me, here's my address, and the address of the meeting house behind Tottenham Court Road.'

He gave me a slip of paper with the addresses written in English script. I struggled to make out the letters, so he read them aloud to me.

'Durleston Buildings, Stepney Green. A great commune,' he said joyfully.

'And this one?'

'*Anonymie*, Windmill Street. Remember? Behind Tottenham Court Road. You'll find me in one or the other.'

Bending, he kissed me on both cheeks.

'Much luck to you, Sophia Kretchevsky, in whatever you do. Always remember, we need intelligent girls like you.'

Again, I blushed. How many times had this happened during the voyage?

'Dov, you've almost persuaded me to stay, but can't I join the movement when I reach New York?'

His face was full of amusement as he smiled down at me.

'Of course you can. Besides, you'll be with your brother.'

Such a wait in the hold before we could disembark, because the cargo of wood came first, and that was more important than all of us. Then porters ran in, grabbing at our trunks and people became very agitated, I included, unable to understand what they were saying or where they were taking our precious belongings. Everything calmed down when two English men descended the stairs and spoke to us in German and Yiddish.

They explained they came from something called the London Shelter. This was a temporary hostel, where immigrants of all religions and nationalities could stay until they found their families or lodgings, or continued onward to wherever they were going.

'Maybe some of you know of us already?' one of them asked. He had twinkling blue eyes and a small reddish moustache. He was probably the age of my father. 'It's an arrangement we've made with the shipping lines,' he continued. 'That way, you won't be fleeced by agents or porters because we have a list of all the travellers on every ship.'

He waved a wad of papers in front of us.

'The Shelter is open to all,' continued the other man. 'But it has facilities for even the most observant amongst you.'

They went from person to person, checking their lists, asking for details, noting them down in little notebooks, telling those who required it to wait at a certain point on the quay when we disembarked. When I told them my plans, one of them still jotted something down in his book, with its grey, water-marked cover.

'In case,' he said, smiling at me.

The porters, now waiting respectfully until they'd finished speaking, were working with them, so there was nothing to fear. At long last, we could leave the ship. We all walked slowly down the ramp and onto the quay, our legs unsteady, wobbling after so many days at sea. I breathed in the sooty smell of London! Amongst the small crowd of people waiting for their family, I searched for Sasha, but couldn't see him. He must be late. Dov had already waved goodbye and left.

The porters pushed their carts down the ramp, waiting in one area for those people who would doubtless be going to this Shelter. Just as in Petersburg, the noise was immense, shouting, banging, birds wheeling and shrieking, people calling to each other, and the thump of water and the clanging of bales being lifted and dropped. I was surrounded by noise and confusion.

I went to an empty space near the back of the wharf, hoping Sasha wouldn't miss me there. A porter came up to me, talking so fast, so unintelligibly, I shook my head, almost in tears. How could I speak to this man? Where was Sasha? What could I do? The man somehow knew the trunk was mine. Maybe the rest had been claimed. With huge arms he lifted it off the cart, as I might have picked up a jewellery box, and placing it next to me, he grinned, tipping his cap and walked off, whistling.

The people dispersed. I looked this way and that, my heart beating faster and faster. All the passengers had gone. Something must have happened to delay him, I told myself. He'd surely be there soon. But now a man was approaching me, and it wasn't Sasha. Something in his manner, the way he looked around shiftily, made me apprehensive. Just as he neared me, smiling strangely and talking in a Yiddish I barely understood, two women marched towards us. Peering at them, he turned, then dashed in front of me, and disappeared behind a pyramid of wooden boxes further along the quay.

The women walked swiftly towards me. I could see they were well dressed in sober blues and grey. The one in the grey dress, wearing a matching hat, with a tiny veil over her eyes, spoke first.

'Yiddish? German? English?'

'I'm Russian,' I answered, 'but I also speak German and Yiddish.'

'Are you all right?' she asked, peering at me.

I wasn't sure what they meant and as I was anxiously waiting for Sasha to come, I only nodded.

'Good. He didn't say anything to you? You see, we're from the Ladies' Protection Society,' she continued. 'I'm Mrs Hendon and my friend is Mrs Lucas. We must have arrived in the nick of time.'

'Sophia Kretchevsky,' I said, wonderingly.

We shook hands.

'Are you all alone?' asked Mrs Lucas.

When I explained my predicament, Mrs Hendon looked around.

'It's rather late for anyone to arrive now.' She stopped. 'And that man ...'

'Not a good place for a young woman to wait unaccompanied,' interrupted Mrs Lucas. 'You see what happened? But be assured, we're here to help you.'

'Thank you,' I said, even more bemused.

'I think, my dear, that it would be wise if we took you to the London Shelter.'

'The London Shelter? No, I can't possibly go there. What if my brother comes and I've gone. How would he know I was there?'

They looked at each other.

'Listen, Miss Kretchevsky, we'll wait with you for half an hour, in case your brother's been detained. But if he doesn't come, we have to make sure you're safe.'

'You can't possibly stay here. Surely that's what he would want?' said the other lady, with such an air of authority, I knew she was used to giving orders. 'Your trunk will follow you.'

'But how shall I find Sasha?' I whispered.

'They'll help you at the Shelter. They're very experienced in all this,' said Mrs Lucas, who wasn't so fierce.

They stood guard over me until Mrs Hendon lifted a watch from her bag and consulted it.

'It's time. We shall go.'

Full of trepidation, I let them take me to the London Shelter, only twenty minutes' walk from the docks. Once inside, they told a woman sitting behind a heavy walnut desk, what had happened, then shook my hand again and left, wishing me well.

She was called Mrs Haber. A warm, cheerful lady with thick red hair coiled round like Mama's, and the lovely, white skin that goes with it. She didn't wear a scarf or a *sheitel,* a wig.

'Born here,' she said. 'I'm a cockney. My family come here in 1850 and I went to school just down the road. Best country in the world, I always say.'

She spoke all the languages under the sun, looked after the desk, supervised the laundry, and knew everyone who lived round about, and their families, and where they'd come from. We walked up the stairs together, to a room I'd share with three other ladies. There were curtains for privacy around each bed.

'This one's yours. I bet you're dropping.'

I thanked her.

She laughed at me.

'You've met some of the rich ladies today. Almost aristocracy. Saved you from a fate worse than death.'

I stared at her.

She laughed again.

'The White Slave Trade. Prostitution!'

'I didn't know,' I murmured.

'Very upper-class, but kindly. You wouldn't expect them good ladies to go down the docks whenever a ship arrives, but they do. You're not the first girl they've brought to me.'

So. Mrs Haber gave me tickets for meals, and the most wonderful thing, told me when I could take bath, my first in weeks. A bath! At last, soothed by the beautiful hot water, the vista of the white porcelain, the shiny taps, the cleanliness, I began to feel more like myself. She also convinced me that I would have no problem finding my brother.

'It happens again and again,' she said. 'Tomorrow, I'll draw you a little map; I'll send someone with you, and you'll find him, sure as eggs is eggs.'

After all, I slept soundly my first night in England.

Next morning I showed Mrs Haber Sasha's address.

'Goolden Street? Just by Petticoat Lane, runs parallel really. Only a few minutes' walk from here. But, Sophia, I've nobody to go with you now.'

'I can't wait,' I said. 'I speak a few words of English, I'm sure I'll find it.'

She couldn't dissuade me.

'You cross a great roundabout over the Commercial Road. Take the road on the left, Whitechapel Street, and facing you, going up, is Goolden Street. Be very careful.'

She gave me a card with the name of the Shelter on it, and the address, in case I got lost, and off I went.

I might have been back in Russia. Shops with names and goods written in Hebrew or Russian script; people selling cucumbers and beigels, vorsht; men with long beards, women with scarves. But also as I walked, I noticed people of all nationalities, English, German, African, or so I thought, all in this part of London, what Mrs Haber called the East End. With a lighter heart, I followed the map until I reached 37 Goolden St, a flat on the ground floor of a gaunt block of flats.

A woman came to the door, her hair drawn tightly back from her face. She didn't seem very old, maybe in her thirties. When I spoke to her, she called her husband, working in the next room. He walked stiffly, with difficulty.

'Sasha Kretchevsky,' I repeated.

He frowned, looked at me sorrowfully, sighed.

'Too late, Miss Kretchevsky. I'm very sorry.'

'How do you mean, too late?'

Caught by a deep, hacking cough, he turned away to wipe his mouth. It was some moments before he could speak again. Reaching over the fireguard, strewn with drying baby clothes, he took a letter from behind the clock and handed it to me.

'He left last week for America. Here. This is the letter he asked me to give you.'

I must have gone white. I swayed and clung to the door. The woman rushed forward and gripping my arms, dragged me in, pushing me into a poor, lumpy armchair by the fire.

'Some tea,' she cried. 'Take a glass of tea.'

Lifting a black steaming kettle from the hob, she poured water into a teapot. Within seconds, I was holding a glass of hot tea in my hands.

'Sugar, sugar,' she urged, lifting lumps with the sugar tongs, and dropping them into my hand. For some time, I lay back in the chair, even though the tea was beginning to revive me. The man went back to his work, the woman watched me anxiously. Finally, I took courage and opened the letter.

This is what he wrote:

*My Dearest Sophia,*

*Forgive me, but I've had to go without you. The agent swindelled us. Only one ticket was valid for America, even though I'd paid for two. It was for a Cunard liner, leaving earlier than we'd planned. Of course, I didn't know. I had to take the ship or we'd have lost all the money. I'll send you a ticket from New York to this address. They are very kind people. Mr Anofsky helped me when I was looking for a room. They'll advise you.*

*Your heart-broken brother, Sasha.*

Then I read it to Mrs Anofsky.

'Tsk, tsk,' she said, nodding, frowning. 'What *ganufs*. Thieves, the lot of them.'

Again, she called her husband.

'How many times have I heard this,' said the man, gazing at me with such sadness I might have been his daughter.

'Shame we haven't room for you, but this is all we have. Two rooms – the boys sleep in here with my husband, the girls in the back room with me,' said the woman, just as sadly.

I shook my head.

'Thank you. You've been so kind. I don't want to trouble you any more.'

'We'll look out for his letter,' added the man. 'It'll be some weeks from now.'

Just as I was leaving, Mrs Anofsky asked me where I was staying, what I was going to do.

'I'm at the London Shelter,' I said.

'Good. They'll advise you. But if you ever need anything, anything at all, please come and see us.'

What could I do? *What Is To Be Done?* The words of the socialist book sprang into my mind, as I returned to the London Shelter. And the answer? Now I would certainly look for Dov Feldman. Maybe I'd also find work until my brother sent me a ticket. After all, that could be months away.

When I showed Dov's addresses to Mrs Haber and Mr Fuchs, who worked with her, they weren't so happy.

'We will tell you where it is, of course,' said Mrs Haber reluctantly, 'but do you really need to go there?'

'He promised to help me.'

'We can help you. We can help you find a room, work. What can you do?'

'I've done some teaching. I could translate, write letters.'

'Then you won't starve.'

'But still,' I said wistfully, 'now my brother has gone, I know nobody at all in this country. I am quite alone, except for him.'

'It's not such a good thing for a young girl to get involved with those people,' said Mr Fuchs, who supervised the kitchens and handled the problems Mrs Haber couldn't deal with. 'Not that I don't agree with their politics. I do. Most of us round here are members of the unions. Our lives are improving, thanks to people like them.'

'Then why not?' I demanded.

'It's ... it's their morals, see,' said Mrs Haber doubtfully. 'Look, you can go, but promise me you'll come straight back. I'll be waiting for you. Don't let me down. We don't want no more trouble do we?'

And so it was, on my second, or was it my third day in London, I found myself on top of an omnibus, travelling down Tottenham Court Road. I'd almost recovered from my shock of not finding Sasha, the sun was shining, it was warm, everyone walked through London with a smile on their face, it seemed to me. I was enchanted.

Windmill Street was as Dov had said, just off the main road. The meeting house wasn't hard to find. I pushed open the door and saw many people sitting at tables, smoking, drinking tea. There were bookshelves lining the back wall. In the centre of everything, facing me, was Dov, laughing that familiar laugh. A young woman, wearing a bright red dress, was sitting on one side of him, leaning her head on his shoulder. On the other was a handsome, young man with deep blue eyes, wearing a black waistcoat and jacket, as smartly dressed as Dov.

I was completely taken aback by this girl leaning over Dov, and the way she gazed up at him. I wanted to open the door, run to Tottenham Court Road, jump on the omnibus and get back to the East End as fast as I could. In the safety of the London Shelter, I would hide myself away and cry my heart out into the pillow.

But he saw me.

He leaped up, shouting, 'Sophia, you've changed your mind.'

Reaching me, he kissed me six times, just as Sasha would have done. Interrupted in their discussions and conversations by Dov's excitement, everyone in the room looked up expectantly. Before I could begin to speak, explain why I was there, Dov shouted, 'I want you all to meet our latest recruit to the cause. The girl from Archangelsk, Sophia Kretchevsky.'

# About the Authors

BASHIR AHMED fled persecution in Afghanistan and arrived in the UK three years ago, after a journey lasting several months. He is currently attending college and hopes that he can continue to write.

MULI AMAYE was born in a cottage flat, in the corner of a tiny cul-de-sac in Burnage, Manchester. She went to Wright Robinson High School, leaving to start work at 16. She worked in offices over the next 20 years, from solicitors to housing to publishers of a dog's weekly newspaper. She went to Manchester Metropolitan University in 1998 to study English and discovered a love of writing that complemented her lifelong love of reading. An MA in Creative Writing followed and after a two-year break, working in the community, she began her PhD in Creative Writing at Lancaster University . Her writing interests are very much centred around Manchester, migration, memory and notions of home, and this is incorporated into the workshops and projects she is involved in throughout Greater Manchester.

VALERIE BARTLEY was born in 1943 in Jamaica, the eldest of Lattemore and Elsaida Hancels' eight children. Life was hard in Bois Content and she had to do many chores before going to school. Her teenage years were unhappy. At sixteen she met Eric, who was about to emigrate to England. They kept in touch and when she was eighteen she came to England and married him. There was hardship to begin with, and she was homesick. She has three children, and has always interested in writing stories. Valerie's life has never been easy, but writing is her therapy.

MAGGIE COBBETT, born in Leeds, crossed the Pennines to study modern languages at the University of Manchester. Despite the Sixties being in full swing at the time, she managed to do enough work to get her degree and later qualify as a teacher. This led to a succession of posts in the UK and abroad, with most of the proceeds spent on travelling until marriage and motherhood slowed her down. Now retired from the world of education and settled in North Yorkshire with her family, she works part time as a television extra and helps to run a social group for learning disabled adults.

MATTHEW CURRY was born in Manchester. He has self-published several collections of poetry, including *Fourteen, City Sonnets, Yevgeny, U Evol, Ordinary Time* and *Mumbo Jumbo*. Currently he is training to be a teacher of mathematics. He lives in Old Trafford with his wife and three of his four children.

NICOLA DALY was born in 1974 in Dewsbury, West Yorkshire. However, most of her formative years were spent in Chester. In 1997 she graduated from the North East Wales Institute of Higher Education with a BA (Hons) degree in English and history. After many unrewarding jobs and further qualification she began teaching ESOL and creative writing at further education colleges in the north-west. She has had many poems published in small press magazines such as *Rialto, The Shop* and *Mslexia*.

She has also had short stories published in two Honno press anthologies. She has been writing for some years.

ROWENA FAN (from Manchester, twentysomething) grew up in the north of the city. She later studied English at Manchester University. She has had work published previously with Commonword in the *Hair* anthology and with Penguin books in their *Decibel* anthology. Her other ventures include photography, commercial writing and writing for various blogs. She is currently working on a full-length novel whilst taking care of five cats, and building up a very impressive handbag collection.

OVIE JOBOME was born in Warri, Nigeria, where he spent his formative years. He also completed most of his education and early career in Nigeria. He moved to the UK in the mid-nineties, a change which broadened his career and worldview considerably. His interest in writing started at a very early age, though it took the sharp edge of real-life experience to hone his writing craft. His diasporic credentials are clearly visible in the duality he richly portrays in his writings. He also enjoys reading.

KATH MCKAY was born in Liverpool, studied in Belfast and London and lives in Leeds. Recent work appears in *The North, Smiths Knoll, Mslexia, Rialto* and *Stories from the City* . She has published one novel, one poetry collection, and short stories, poetry and journalism in anthologies, magazines and newspapers. She taught at London, Leeds and Bradford universities and now teaches creative writing at Hull University. She has written on the swimming pools of Leeds, regeneration in East Hull, and teeth. She worked as a Crossing Borders mentor for Lancaster University (www.crossing-borders-african writing.org) and also worked with Finnish writers on a publication, *Interland* (Smith Doorstop). She is completing a short story collection.

VIJAY MEDTIA is a novelist and a short-story writer. He was born in Greater Manchester and has travelled frequently to India, which inspires most of his fiction.

His debut novel *The House of Subadar*, was published in 2006 by Arcadia. It was short listed for the Glen Dimplex New Writers Award – Dublin 2007. This gave him much needed encouragement in his writing. Presently working flat out on his second and third novels, plus writing several new short stories, he feels very glad to be accepted in this collection. He wishes to thank Corinne Fowler for her editing and comments and Peter Kalu for his suggestions. www.vijaymedtia. co.uk

TARIQ MEHMOOD's first novel, *Hand on the Sun* (Penguin, 1983), focused on the problems of Asian youths in the 1970s. His second novel, *While There Is Light* (Comma, 2003), is a fictionalised account of his own arrest on charges of terrorism in 1981, in a case known as the Bradford 12. Tariq co-directed the award-winning documentary *Injustice*. He writes in both English and Pothowari, his mother tongue, and is a founder of the Pothowari-Pahari language movement. Tariq has also had two children's books published. One of these, *Pahi Adha* (trans. Half Brother), has recently been made into a film.

MARTIN DE MELLO was named after a church visible from the window of the room he was born in. He remembered it to be a large church as a child but on returning thirty years later found it in fact to be rather small. He has had the same experience with Cadbury's creme eggs. Martin has been writing for several years and has had work published in a variety of anthologies. He lives in Manchester and would like the opportunity to travel more.

QAISRA SHAHRAZ was born in Pakistan but has lived in Manchester since the age of nine. She is a critically acclaimed novelist and scriptwriter. Her novels *The Holy Woman* and *Typhoon* have been translated into several languages and become part of major literary festivals. Her drama serial *The Heart Is It* won two TV Awards in Pakistan. Her award-winning short stories are studied in schools and colleges, especially *A Pair of Jeans* in Germany. Her non-fiction work includes a teacher guide book, *Emerging India*, for German teachers and students. She has just completed her third novel.

SUE STERN was born in London but has lived in Manchester since 1945. She had always written – diaries, stories, plays in French for the children she taught – until the discovery of Commonword, in the nineties, inspired her to write seriously. She has published poems and short fiction in Britain and America, and has an MA in writing children's fiction (Manchester Metropolitan University). Deeply affected by her radical upbringing – grandparents Russian, Jewish anarchists; parents committed socialists, sometime fellow travellers – she has explored themes of alienation in her work. Her latest novel for children, the story of Mancunian, Rafi Brown, dyslexic but brilliant cartoonist, and his friend, Candy Floss, child carer, reflects on the joys and terrors of children forced to 'bunk off school', but ends happily!

Kim Wiltshire was brought up in Devon and Dorset, the family touring to many seaside resorts and towns with her father, who was a musician. She currently lives in Sale with her husband, CB, and works a variety of jobs, including teaching creative writing at MMU and for the Open University, working as a freelance community artist and running the community arts department for Lime Arts and Health. She is in the final year of her PhD at Lancaster University, exploring The Loser as a form of interim masculinity through contemporary texts. Sometimes she has time to write.

Hua Zi: Born in China shortly before the ten-year Cultural Revolution (1966-1976), she grew up and pursued both undergraduate and postgraduate studies in China. She loves Chinese literature and is proud of her Chinese cultural heritage, hence the name Hua Zi (from *Hua Xia Zi Sun* – meaning *the child of China)*. She has lived in the UK for some two decades and now lives, with her husband, in Manchester where she enjoys the cultural and creative diversity of her adopted city. But being shy in nature, she often retreats to the fictional world and feels at ease there.